VEGEMORPHS

The Fungus Among Us

Leif E. Green

Chapter One

I can't tell you my first name—or my last name, either. And I can't tell you where I live. But I might be lying in your refrigerator's vegetable bin or in the produce section of your local supermarket right now.

So let me ask you—no, beg you—please, *please* don't put any vegetables into a zipper bag. I know this sounds crazy, but let me explain.

I can't tell you anything about me or my friends, because then the Jerkks would find us. They are the fungus among us. They are trying to decay the whole world—all the vegetables and people.

It's not easy for me to keep secrets. . . . Okay, I'll tell you this much. The town I live in is a small one. To tell you any more would be dangerous. If any of the head fungi (I mean the fungi in charge, not the ones that grow on someone's head) got hold of me, the results would be, well, blistering.

I can only tell you my code name and those of my friends who are fighting the fungus. My code name is Kyle—I mean, *Kale*—and I'm a boy. The code names for the rest of us are: Carrot, who is a boy; Tomato, a boy who is my best friend; Radish, my cousin, who is a girl; and Olive, a girl I sort of like.

Radish isn't a close cousin as far as the family goes. According to my mom, she's my fourth cousin once removed (whatever that means).

None of us are what you'd call normal—at least not in Br—*Whoops!* I almost told you the name of our town. Most of the kids in town are the plaid-shirt-and-jeans type. And some of the guys are real jerks—I mean, jocks.

Not that there's anything wrong with that. But Carrot, Tomato, Radish, Olive, and I are different. We like to wear funky clothes, listen to alternative music, and do crazy things. So depending on who you are, we're either the coolest kids or the biggest geeks in school.

We think we're the coolest. But most of the rest of the kids don't. Especially Biff R—*Whoops!* I almost forgot, no last names—and his bunch of brain-dead bullies.

Sometimes I think back to before it happened—the thing that changed our lives forever, changed us from kids who were either geeky or cool to kids who were really different. It seems like yesterday—or the day before yesterday.

I'll tell you one thing, though. You'll probably never say *veg out* again after you hear my story. Not once you realize that some people veg out for a little while—but some of them veg out . . . forever.

I just want everyone to be on guard. I also want to tell you not to eat your vegetables. Any one of them could be someone you know. They might even start talking to you.

Meanwhile, my friends and I have got to fight the fungus. And the members of the Vegetable Kingdom—the super vegetables—will help us.

Chapter Two

Here's how it all started. I—Kale—was hanging out at the bingo parlor at the mall along with Carrot, Tomato, Radish, and Olive. I guess I'd better explain, because you're probably asking yourself: *Why were they hanging out with a bunch of old ladies at a bingo parlor at the mall when they could have been hanging out* at *the mall?*

The answer is that every time the Biff Bunch caught us at the mall, they chased us and chucked apple cores at us. I don't know how they got so many apple cores, or why they carried them around the mall hoping they would see us, but they did. Who can understand bullies?

After the tenth time it happened, we gave up and started going to the bingo parlor. To tell you the truth, it was really a goof.

The bingo parlor was started by a farmer named Withers. Yes, Withers was his first name. I'd like to tell

6

you his full name because it's really funny . . . but I can't.

Anyway, old ladies were always after Withers, inviting him over for dinner, bringing him cookies they'd just baked, and pestering him in general. So Withers built this bingo parlor to give them something to do.

Withers's Bingo Palace is packed just about every night of the week. The funniest thing is, you can't even win anything. All you get to do is shout, "Bingo!" But the old ladies seem to get a bang out of that.

Anyway, the joke turned out to be on Withers— because after he opened the bingo parlor, even more old ladies were pounding on his door. By the way, I know all this because my brother, Bryce, worked for him. But I'll tell you more about that later.

"Bingo!" Tomato had just shouted before we decided to leave.

Oh, forget it. I can't go on with this code-name business. I just feel too silly calling my best friend *Tomato*. It's kind of hard to take my story seriously that way, isn't it? So I'll tell you our first names.

I told you I couldn't keep secrets very well. I just hope you can. Please don't tell anyone else our first names. And I mean *anyone*.

You already know my name is *Kyle*, not Kale. Tomato's name is *Tommy*—he's my best friend. Carrot is *Cary*, another guy who's a good friend. The two girls in the group are *Randi* and *Olivia*, not Radish and Olive.

So now you know our names. Anyway, we'd run out of money for game cards, and it was getting late, so we decided we might as well leave.

Now we had to make a decision: whether to walk down the streets to get to our houses, which would take us about forty minutes, or to take a shortcut through Withers's field.

Withers's field was kind of scary. No matter what he tried, nothing would grow there but stinkweeds. Everything else *withered*. He was a nice old guy, if a little strange. He had a lot of money he kept stashed in his mattress—but he sure didn't get it from farming.

"Let's go for it. Let's go through Withers's field," said Cary. Cary is like that: daring.

All the girls in school were always offering to do Cary's homework for him. Not that Cary needed any help. He's probably some kind of genius. Girls always blushed and giggled when he walked by, too. I guess you'd say Cary was a really good-looking guy. But Cary didn't seem to notice all the attention from the girls. Lots of times he seemed lost in his own thoughts. He never said much.

It was like Cary never even had to study. He could read something once—real fast, you know, like he was just scanning it. Then he could recite it word for word. It was amazing.

The first time I met Cary was at Tommy's house. Cary had his head stuck in the clothes dryer, and it was on. Cary had just washed his hair, and he said his family had just moved in and they couldn't find their blow dryer. He's always had his own way of doing things.

"Well, what are we standing around for?" Cary

asked. "I'm going through Withers's field. Who's coming with me?"

The rest of us exchanged glances. Cary had given us a dare, and none of us was the type to back down.

"I'm in," said Tommy.

"So am I," I told him.

"Me, too," Randi and Olivia said at practically the same time. I never doubted the two of them for a minute. They are two fierce items. Randi is totally into fashion—especially hats. She's already had offers to model, but she's not interested. Randi may look like a magazine cover girl, but she's a pretty deep thinker, too.

Olivia is Hispanic, and also drop-dead gorgeous, though in a different way from Randi. Olivia is usually dressed in something like motorcycle boots, ripped jeans, and a T-shirt. Olivia's mom and dad run a local greenhouse, and Olivia spends a lot of time talking to the plants.

I guess I have a bit of a crush on Olivia, but it's kind of hard to get close to her. One reason is that Olivia likes plants, flowers, and vegetables better than she likes people. Anyway, I wouldn't recommend that anyone get on the wrong side of Randi or Olivia. In an instant, either one of them can turn from a vision of beauty into your worst possible nightmare.

So there we were, taking a forbidden shortcut across Withers's field at night. Everyone but Cary was trying to pretend we weren't scared when weird things started to happen. Just as we reached the edge of Withers's property, something overhead sprayed the

9

whole area with an awful-smelling, powdery kind of stuff.

Olivia looked closely at the powdery things as they drifted down. "Maybe they're spores," she whispered. "They're like seeds, except they don't produce plants— they make fungi."

"I don't care what they are," I said, practically choking on the stench. "Let's get out of here." I turned to go, but Cary grabbed my sleeve.

"Look up there," he said, pointing into the sky. I looked, but I didn't see anything unusual. In addition to practically being a genius, Cary has this amazing eyesight. He could probably tell what time it is by looking from an airplane at somebody's watch on the ground.

One by one, Tommy, Randi, and Olivia told Cary that they didn't see anything either . . . yet. The stench in the air got worse, but Cary kept insisting that we couldn't go anywhere because this thing was getting closer and closer.

And then, finally, I saw it. We all saw it.

You've probably heard or read descriptions of flying saucers. They're usually disc-shaped, or pod-shaped, or even sometimes triangles. But I'd never seen anything like what I saw that night . . . floating straight toward *us*.

"Is it a bird?" I wondered aloud.

"Is it a plane?" Tommy asked.

"No!" Cary said in a hushed voice. "It's not a flying saucer, either. I can't believe it, but it's a gigantic, flying *mushroom!"*

Chapter Three

"It's a *Portobello* mushroom," Olivia explained. "They make very good appetizers."

This was no ordinary flying Portobello mushroom, though. Uh, wait a minute. There is no such thing as an ordinary flying Portobello mushroom.

Anyway, this had lights all around it, and the stem was covered with some kind of protective armor. Suddenly the bottom of the stem opened like it was a hatch or something. Whoever was inside dumped another mass of puffy, powdery little things out of the hatch, and they all fell on Withers's field.

"They're spores, all right," Olivia whispered. "I bet they're mushroom spores. Mushrooms are fungi, you know." After that, we all started gagging. The worst stink I had ever smelled in my life was hanging in the air. It hugged everything it touched, pouring into my nose, my mouth . . . even my ears.

Only Cary wasn't gagging. He was just staring up at that big mushroom in the sky. "I wonder where that came from," he said. He looked awestruck.

"Yuck!" I sputtered between bouts of retching. "Let's get out of here." I started to leave, but Cary took hold of my sleeve with his hand again. As if it were all planned, I stayed there with him.

And it was grand just to stand there and watch the great mushroom slow down. It was gradually descending toward the earth.

Then something else weird happened. All at once, I didn't feel sick anymore. My stomach was calm.

Tommy, Randi, and Olivia had been doubled over with the smell, but now they stood up straight.

"I feel wonderful," said Olivia.

"Never felt better," said Tommy.

"I hear that," said Randi with a nod.

Randi was just using an expression, but I really did hear something. A strange voice was talking to us.

I turned around to see where the voice was coming from and gasped. A stalk of broccoli about six feet high was shuffling toward me. Cary, Tommy, Randi, and Olivia were looking at it, too.

Did you ever hear the expression *Pinch me, I must be dreaming?* Well, I pinched myself—hard.

"Ow!" I heard the screech of pain come out of my mouth. That hurt. I must not have been dreaming!

The stalk of broccoli had two shiny red eyes just below what looked like a huge, green head of curly hair. It was just the top part of the broccoli, of course, but since I'd never seen broccoli with a face before, it was hard not to think of it as hair.

Here's something else that was weird. This broccoli had tentacle-like arms and legs at the bottom of the stalk.

The broccoli stood in front of us. "I am Prince Brassica Oleracea Italica Cruciferae," it said. Well, I guess it must have been a *he*, because a prince is always a *he*. "You may call me Prince Brassica," he said.

I tried to say something but couldn't. I just kept moving my mouth, but no words came out. Then, finally, I found my voice.

"Who . . . are you?" I stammered.

"The Prince of the Vegetable Kingdom," he replied.

Olivia turned green. "You can talk . . . and I've been eating vegetables all my life," she gasped.

The broccoli gave a dismissive wave of his hand that actually looked regal. "There are vegetables, and then there are *vegetables*. It's like comparing a doll or a department-store mannequin with a human being. They may look a lot alike, but they aren't the same."

"How can we tell the difference?" Cary asked. I had never seen that intense concentration in his eyes before, or heard that heavy tone of voice.

The royal vegetable tilted his curly-topped head. "There's no way to tell, unless you can communicate with us. We of the Vegetable Kingdom don't try to communicate with most humans because it makes us so tired. They haven't got the power to communicate with

13

us on our own level. It's a skill that usually takes a long time to learn.

"But ordinary vegetables *can't* communicate—they just 'veg out,' as you humans say. They have no real consciousness.

"Members of the Vegetable Kingdom can make themselves known to you if you have special powers. Unless they're cut up in a salad, casserole, or side dish first, of course."

I swallowed hard, thinking that perhaps I had eaten one of these creatures before.

It was as if Prince Brassica had read my thoughts. "Don't worry," he said. "The royal vegetables are not usually captured. We grow underground, not above ground, as regular vegetables do. In fact, we have a labyrinth of tunnels right under this field."

Aha! I thought. *That's why nothing ever grows here.*

"That's why nothing ever grows here," said Prince Brassica, echoing my thoughts again. "We don't need sunlight, but we appreciate all of the care, water, and food we've been given. It's made our lives a lot easier."

"But why live underground? Don't you prefer the sun?"

Prince Brassica shook his curly top. "We went into hiding until we could find a way to destroy the fungi that were trying to kill us—the Jerkks. That was on a faraway planet. Now we've come here. So far we've held our own, but it's a constant battle. Every day or so one of us is spotted, wilted, or dried out—killed by the Jerkks."

14

"Where will it all end? When they destroy you?" I asked.

Then Prince Brassica said something that chilled me to the bone. "It won't end there," he said. "The Jerkks aren't only after vegetables. They're after everything on Earth—you, too."

Chapter Four

Prince Brassica drew himself up to his full height. "The Jerkks attack humans as well as vegetables. They live from decay and need hosts to support what they feed on.

"They go from planet to planet. When they arrive, they first make everything rot. Then they rule over the mold and fungus that feed on the remains of the life forms there. When there is nothing more to decay, they move on."

"You mean, they're going to try to make people decay?" Randi asked with a tremor in her voice. For once, Randi didn't seem so tough.

"They have fungi they use for soldiers. They cause diseases you may be familiar with, such as athlete's foot— or worse . . . blisters, rashes, and horrible, oozing sores."

"Stop!" said Olivia. "I can't stand it anymore!"

"Me, either," said Tommy.

"Don't despair. We of the Vegetable Kingdom have vowed to fight the Jerkks wherever they go. We have followed them to dozens of planets throughout the galaxy."

"Have you succeeded?" Tommy asked.

Prince Brassica looked sad. "We lost the last planet," he said.

"What about the one before that?" asked Randi.

Prince Brassica shook his head. "Beaten."

"But you won on the planet before that, right?" Olivia asked eagerly.

Prince Brassica hung his curly head and looked at the ground. "Uh . . . not exactly."

My stomach was churning. I was feeling sick. "Um, exactly how many times have you defeated the Jerkks? How many planets have you saved?"

An awful silence hung in the air. We all waited for the answer. Then we waited some more.

"Let me guess," I finally said. "What you're not saying is that you've never won. You haven't saved a single planet from the Jerkks, have you?"

Something like a little sob escaped from Prince Brassica. "All right, all right, we've never won. In the end, we always turn and run, and they cover everything with mold," he said. His voice took on a whiny tone. "Do you know what that does to my self-esteem?" he said. "I feel like a joke."

"Now, now." Olivia put her arm around him. "Do they have therapists in the Vegetable Kingdom? You need to feel better about yourself."

"Cut it out, Olivia," I said. I pointed to the big mushroom in the sky. "We're being attacked." I turned to Prince Brassica. "Pull yourself together and help us. What can we do about this?"

Just then, a group of large asparagus marched across the field toward us. It was one strange sight, I have to tell you. Just try to imagine having about seven asparagus eight or nine feet tall coming toward you.

"You are an alien being!" said one in a voice that made my eardrums pound.

"Away with you! Back away from Prince Brassica!" rumbled another.

"Get lost!" commanded a third.

Suddenly Prince Brassica turned around and faced the head asparagus. "Back off, Jack!" he snapped. "Don't forget who's running the show here!"

Wow, was I relieved. In an instant, Prince Brassica had turned from a whiner to a leader. Maybe he could help us after all.

The group of Asparagus Officinalis withered a little and looked embarrassed.

Prince Brassica stood up straight. "The Jerkks are parasites. They live off and try to control whatever they invade. Watch for people who scratch. Watch for blisters and deformed fingernails. And watch how people act."

"How they *act?*" we all asked in chorus. "How do they act?"

Prince Brassica looked up at the mushroom ship. "You'll know in a minute. They'll act like the creatures that get out of the ship that's going to land any second now." He paused and watched the mushroom descend.

"I can give you special powers that no humans have," Prince Brassica said after a moment. For an instant he looked proud. "I can teach you how to change—morph—into members of the Vegetable Kingdom. I can show you how to become vegetables!"

Tommy rolled his eyes. "Terrific. I could turn into a tomato. That ought to frighten the pants off anybody."

I had to admit it didn't sound like much of a scare tactic.

Prince Brassica looked quite indignant. "*I* am a vegetable," he said. "But it's you humans who are running this planet—not vegetables. And you're running it into the ground, I might add."

"Don't be rude," I whispered to Tommy.

"Sorry," Tommy said reluctantly. "Please tell us what we can do as vegetables."

"As a vegetable, you can communicate with the members of the Vegetable Kingdom. As a vegetable, you can hide. The Jerkks and the humans who are taken over by them won't be able to tell if you're a real vegetable or not. You can zap them with vitamins and minerals."

I let out a long sigh. It was better than nothing. "So how do we become vegetables?"

"Once I give you the special power, all you have to do is smell a vegetable deeply, and you will discover its essence. Your body will be in tune with the vegetable. Then, once you put your mind to it, you can turn into one.

"You won't be ordinary vegetables," the broccoli

told us. "Not only will you have the powers of members of the Vegetable Kingdom, but the vegetable DNA will combine with your human DNA. You'll have the combined powers of both species. Then you can use them to fight the Jerkks."

We all stood there, speechless. I don't know what was going through everyone else's mind, but I'd guess my friends were thinking what I was—that maybe we'd eaten something at the bingo parlor that was making us feel like we'd fallen down the rabbit hole and gone through the looking glass in *Alice in Wonderland*.

Chapter Five

"**H**urry and make up your minds," urged Prince Brassica. He shook his curly broccoli head impatiently. "Are you going to save your planet or not?" He pointed toward the sky. "The Jerkks will be here any minute."

"Okay, okay," I said suddenly. I didn't even realize the words had come out. It was like I hadn't engaged my brain before putting my mouth in gear. But once I had said I'd go along with Prince Brassica's plan, I felt in my bones that there was no turning back.

"Are you with me, everyone?" I asked. I figured they'd all fall in behind me, because I'm sort of the leader of the group.

"Nah," said Tommy. "Not interested."

"No way," said Randi.

"We're going to wake up and find out this was all some crazy dream," said Olivia.

It was Cary who helped me turn things around. "If

21

we're only dreaming, we don't have anything to worry about," he said. "I say we go for it. I mean, the bingo parlor is getting a little stale, right?"

"Okay, whatever you say, Cary!" Tommy declared enthusiastically.

"Right behind you, man," said Randi.

"Same here." Olivia nodded.

"Glad I made you come to your senses," I said. I turned to Prince Brassica. "Now what?"

"Wait just a minute," cautioned Prince Brassica. "I should probably tell you that this can be dangerous. If you remain a vegetable longer than the recommended cooking time, you will remain a vegetable for all eternity."

The ship was rapidly approaching. "Fine," I said, trying to be polite and keep the impatience out of my voice.

Prince Brassica pointed to a hole in the ground. "Squirm on down there," he said to me. "There is a network of big tunnels underneath this field. That's where we've been hiding. Once you get down the main tunnel, you'll come to a fork."

"You mean the tunnel will branch into two?" I asked.

Prince Brassica looked puzzled. "What are you talking about? I mean a fork. Later on, you'll come to a spoon and a knife. You make a right at the fork, go straight until you come to the spoon, then make a left until you come to the knife. My headquarters is just behind it, inside the big cup and saucer."

"Um, okay," I said. I could see Tommy was barely able to control his laughter.

Prince Brassica glared at Tommy, then turned back to me. "Pull the handle on the cup, and the door will open. On the other side, you'll find a big room. Go in there and open the refrigerator. Bring me back the bottle of salad dressing you find inside."

Chapter Six

I felt like my feet were glued to the ground. "Uh . . . maybe this isn't such a good idea," I said. "We're just a bunch of kids."

I was still trying to believe that I was the leader of the group. I figured I should introduce a little bit of caution and reason into this whole situation. I wanted my friends to listen to my words of wisdom, to stop and think.

Tommy rolled his eyes. "Don't be such a wimp," he said.

"Yeah," said Randi.

"Get down there and get that salad dressing," said Olivia.

Cary looked me straight in the eye. "You're going to do just what Prince Brassica said," he told me. His gaze was hypnotic.

Cary pointed up into the sky. The lights around the

base of the mushroom were getting closer and closer. "Get going, Kyle," he said.

Without another word, I headed down the hole. It was scary in there. It was dark, and I could feel ants crawling on me.

Pretty soon the tunnel got bigger. I stood upright and brushed myself off. After a while, I came to the fork. It was a big one—it looked like an antique, but my guess is that it was probably stainless steel. How else could it not rust down there in all that moisture?

Beyond the fork, I quickly reached the spoon and the knife. Then I came to the big room that Prince Brassica had told me about—his home.

I headed for the refrigerator. Before I opened it, I stopped in my tracks.

There were five refrigerator magnets stuck on it. One looked just like Prince Brassica. Another one was just a little smaller. The other three magnets were even smaller. They were all clustered close together.

I wiped a tear from my eye. *These magnets are like a picture of Prince Brassica and his family*, I thought.

All of the magnets were holding up notes. Under Prince Brassica was one that said, *Give kids vitamins Tuesday. Don't forget.*

Mrs. Brassica's note said, *Head-dressing appointment, stalk manicure, Wednesday 3:00. Broccoli Father's Day Friday.*

The three kids were all holding up a single note. It said, *Broccoli Dad's Day Friday. Party for Dad.*

I took a deep breath. Cary and the others were right.

We had to help fight the fungus—not only for humans, but for vegetables everywhere.

I pulled open the refrigerator door. All that was in there were a few jars of vitamins and a single long-necked bottle—the salad dressing.

I grabbed the bottle and scrambled as fast as I could toward the exit. I knew ants were getting all over me and I was muddy and filthy, but I didn't care anymore. Now there were more important things to think about.

I reached the ground just as the giant mushroom was coming in for a landing. I raced over to where my friends were standing with Prince Brassica.

"What took you so long?" Olivia asked.

"No time to be a slowpoke," said Randi.

"Stop bickering!" commanded Prince Brassica. He grasped the dressing with a leafy hand. "Everyone, put your hands on the bottle, close your eyes, and clear your minds."

We all did as he said. Prince Brassica put his leafy hand over ours. I wish I could remember whether the salad dressing was Thousand Island, creamy garlic, or ranch—but I can't. All I remember is that a strange tingle went through my body. I felt a whirl of sensations tumbling over one another. I felt tart and tangy, crisp and cool, hot and spicy, crunchy and mellow—all at once. I guess the best way to describe it is that I felt like I was being tossed by a gigantic fork and spoon, over and over again.

Then, suddenly, the sensation was gone, and I felt better than I had ever felt in my life. It was like I had been all mixed up—and now everything was mixed right. I had been *tossed.*

"Now all you have to do is smell a vegetable deeply to become one with it—to morph into that species of vegetable," said Prince Brassica. "Then just concentrate on being human again, and you can morph back."

The prince looked serious. "You can make other people turn into vegetables, too," he said. "Just keep talking to them constantly in a monotone about the most boring thing you can think of. At the same time, keep a mental picture in your mind of the vegetable you want them to be. Then they will have the same powers you do—the powers of a full member of the Vegetable Kingdom, plus your human powers."

Prince Brassica was speaking faster and faster now. The giant mushroom had touched down on the ground. Its lights were flashing, and a door in the stem was starting to open.

"Never remain a vegetable past the recommended cooking time," Prince Brassica whispered, "or you'll be a vegetable forever."

The door opened, and a creature stepped out of the big Portobello mushroom.

"What cooking time do you mean?" I whispered. "Steamed, stir-fried, boiled, or microwaved?"

"Shhh!" said Prince Brassica. "Here come the slave fungi. Don't say a word and don't sweat—they can't see or hear, but they can smell sweat. If they get hold of you, you'll be itching all over."

27

We all stood still and tried not to sweat. Let me tell you, it wasn't easy, because these were the weirdest things I had ever seen.

They were tall—and sort of lacy-looking. Each had a single eye on a long tentacle that bobbed back and forth. They formed two columns outside the mushroom ship and stood at attention.

It's like they're waiting for the President to get out of Air Force One, I thought. *This is definitely bizarre.*

"Those are the Trichophyton," whispered Prince Brassica. "They aren't usually bad. They are content to live quietly and not cause any trouble. You all probably have some form of Trichophyton on your feet right now."

I gasped.

"Be quiet! Listen to me!" snapped Prince Brassica. "They don't cause problems unless something stirs them up. Then they multiply and attack. They'll give you a terrible case of athlete's foot—dry, cracked skin between your toes and itchy, oozing sores."

That really sounds disgusting, I thought.

"This is the perfect weather for athlete's foot," Prince Brassica continued. "A hot, moist summer. Athlete's foot is highly contagious. You can get it easily from walking barefoot in the bathroom. You can even catch it in the swimming pool.

"These Trichophyton have mutated—changed," he explained. "They're bigger and more powerful than normal Trichophyton. They have been enslaved by the Rubrum fungi. The Rubrum attack both plants and animals. No human or vegetable is safe. They are

28

planning to take over the earth. But these are no ordinary Rubrum. They, too, have mutated. They have amazing powers. We call these fungi *Jerkks*."

Suddenly a huge creature wearing terrible clothes stepped out of the mushroom. I was confused. He looked like Prince Brassica—a broccoli—in a bad outfit.

"I don't get it. He looks like a vegetable," I said.

Prince Brassica stood high on his stalk and shook his curly head. "*No!* That's no vegetable. That's Fun Gus, the only one of the fungi that can morph into a vegetable. Fun Gus is their leader. He's ruthless. And he's probably the biggest Jerkk of all."

Well, Fun Gus may have looked like a broccoli, but he was bigger than Prince Brassica. Way bigger.

Fun Gus scratched his chest with a leafy hand and burped. Then he swaggered toward us.

It was a weird sight. Here was this gigantic broccoli stalk with skinny legs—in high-water pants that revealed his white socks—lurching along.

He was wearing a short-sleeved shirt that practically screamed polyester, and he had a bunch of pens and pencils bulging out of his pocket protector. I couldn't believe he was wearing a clip-on bow tie. He had black-framed glasses that were held together on one side with what looked like a Band-Aid.

"Remain hidden, no matter what happens," said Prince Brassica. "You'll be able to understand what's going on. I've given you that much power already."

A million questions were whirling in my head, but there was no time to ask them.

Prince Brassica stepped out of the shadows and stood in the ray of light projected from the giant mushroom.

"Rubrum! Fun Gus! Biggest Jerkk of all! Here I am!" he said boldly.

The giant broccoli in the stupid outfit took a swig from the bottle of celery tonic he had in his hand. "Well, duh . . ." he said. "Prince Brassica Oleracea Italica, I presume."

Chapter Seven

"**W**hy don't you leave us alone?" said Prince Brassica. "You're nothing but a bunch of bullies."

My heart pounded in my chest. *Uh-oh*, I thought. *Prince Brassica is going into his whiny routine again.*

The Asparagus Officinalis lined up behind him. "Yeah, you're really mean," one of them said.

"Why are you always picking on us?" asked another.

My friends and I exchanged glances.

Fun Gus laughed. It was a human sound—one that wasn't nice to hear. It started as a high-pitched titter. *Teeheeheeheehee.* But the giggles got louder and louder until the creature was guffawing. *Hawhawhawhaw. Teeheehee hawhawhaw.* Then Fun Gus doubled over and slapped his knees. He laughed so hard that he sprayed celery tonic from his nose.

As soon as the Trichophyton soldiers saw what Fun Gus was doing, they imitated his every move, giggling, guffawing, and slapping their knees.

Fun Gus hiccuped a few times and then stopped laughing. He stood up and looked Prince Brassica straight in the eye. "Don't try that 'Mr. Innocent' routine with me. You've helped and healed plenty of the victims of our invasions. We've attempted to invade plenty of hosts, but you have *stalked* us ruthlessly—you and your asparagus soldiers and celery stalkers."

He took another swig of tonic. "You can see what we did to your army. There are dozens of celery stalkers right here in this bottle."

Fun Gus hee-hawed again, and then he turned nasty. He turned from a rich, brilliant green broccoli to a grayish blob. He grew and grew until he towered over Prince Brassica, the Asparagus Officinalis, and even the Trichophyton soldiers. Tentacles sprouted all over him.

Now there was no mistaking his identity. He was no vegetable. He was a *fungus* wearing a bad outfit—a really nasty-looking fungus.

I expected Prince Brassica to start whining again, but he surprised me. In a moment I knew that the whining had been just a ploy.

"Stop showing off!" Prince Brassica thundered in a commanding voice so loud it made my stomach hurt.

"Prepare to be fumigated and exterminated!" shrieked the Asparagus Officinalis.

I covered my nose. Fun Gus smelled horrible. He smelled like the stuff they had just sprayed over Farmer Withers's field, only about a hundred times worse. I gagged silently.

After a few seconds, I was able to control myself. I guess somehow I became used to the smell. But it still gave me the creeps. I felt as if the stench of rot and decay was coating me—that I was breathing it into my lungs. I was being invaded by some horrible stink.

"Where are the rest of your soldiers?" shouted Prince Brassica. "I know you always travel with more than one species."

The three eyes in Fun Gus's "head" cluster of tentacles narrowed menacingly. "They're in the ship. Something up my sleeve, you might say." That awful hee-hawing started again.

It's easy to see why they're called Jerkks, I thought. *This guy is the biggest jerk I've ever met.* I gave a sidelong glance to my friends. I could tell they were thinking the same thing.

Tommy was sneering and holding his nose. Randi had this *I can't believe it* expression on her face. Olivia looked disgusted. For once, Cary didn't look like he was daydreaming. He was totally focused on the Jerkk and his soldiers.

"I was planning to start with the vegetables a little lower down on the food chain and then work up to the members of the Vegetable Kingdom," said Fun Gus, "but I've had a change of plans. I think I'll just rot you first."

"You don't stink enough," retorted Prince Brassica. The Trichophyton and the Asparagus Officinalis both surged forward. Vitamins and minerals shot from the asparagus like gleaming electrical charges.

The Trichophyton were dirty fighters. They didn't fight one on one. They swarmed, hundreds of them attacking each Asparagus Officinalis.

Some of the Asparagus Officinalis glowed for a minute, then turned to powder. A few shrank, but then sprang back to life.

Suddenly a hoard of other beings I didn't recognize poured out of the ship. They were weird-looking like fungi—but somehow different.

"I knew it!" exclaimed Prince Brassica. "Bacteria! Decoys!"

I didn't get to ask what he meant by that, because suddenly the bacteria pounced on the Asparagus Officinalis. It was terrible to watch. The strong, proud stalks grew weak and spongy, softer and softer until they turned brown and collapsed on the ground.

I wanted desperately to help. I knew that Randi and Tommy and Olivia did, too. I had a strange feeling about Cary, though. He was looking at Prince Brassica, and I'd never seen that exact look in his eyes before.

Cary usually looks like he's paying attention to something, but sometimes he's off in his own world. With Cary, you just never know.

In an instant, I was jolted out of my thoughts. The Trichophyton fungi began swarming all over Prince Brassica. Spots began to appear on him.

The royal broccoli didn't give up easily. A blue-green flash snaked from him like lightning. He zapped the Trichophyton soldiers again and again.

But more and more kept coming. I saw the blue-green flash grow dimmer and dimmer. Then I felt a weird sensation in my stomach.

I was sure the broccoli was dying. He was wilting away before my eyes.

Prince Brassica let out an awful scream that made my insides twist. I wanted to throw up but couldn't.

Prince Brassica did, though.

Chapter Eight

When my friends and I saw Prince Brassica throw up, it almost set off a chain reaction. Every one of us felt ill, too.

Look, if you had been in the same situation, I bet you would have felt the same way. For one thing, the stench in the air was awful and getting worse by the minute. The Trichophyton were emitting some awful-smelling gas—and they looked gross, too. Gigantic mold. The bacteria didn't look any better.

Just when I thought it couldn't get any worse, I caught a glimpse of Fun Gus, in his giant, mutated Rubrum form, heading toward Prince Brassica. Now I was completely grossed out—Fun Gus made the Trichophyton and the bacteria look like cuddly, cute stuffed animals by comparison.

Prince Brassica was on the ground, almost completely wilted, when Fun Gus staggered near and stood over him. "You're finished, cousin veg. Your stalk is cooked."

Prince Brassica somehow managed to stand up. The legs on the end of his stalk trembled. But when he spoke, there was no fear in his voice.

"There will be more of us. Maybe not today, maybe not tomorrow, or next week, or next month, or next year—you won't know where, and you won't know when, but we'll fix your wagon. One way or another, we're gonna find ya, we're gonna getcha getcha getcha."

Then, suddenly, Prince Brassica disappeared by pulling himself into a hole in the ground.

"The coward crawled away to die!" bragged Fun Gus. "Have a feast, buds!" he screamed.

The rest of the bacteria and the fungi soldiers began laughing as they swarmed over the Asparagus Officinalis, devouring them. That awful, nerdish hee-hawing filled the air.

Then, all at once, the Trichophyton turned toward us. They finally realized we were there.

Cary, Randi, Olivia, Tommy, and I all turned pale with fear. "Our stalks are cooked," muttered Tommy.

"Let's get out of here," Randi suggested.

That's exactly what we did. We ran, with the stink of the moldy oldies right behind us.

We ran across Farmer Withers's field. As I slogged through the mud, I ran so hard that my lungs burned. I thought they would burst.

Cary reached Farmer Withers's house first. He jerked open the door and ran inside.

Old Farmer Withers was dressed in spandex shorts and a tank top. He was doing jumping jacks and staring at an exercise show on his black-and-white portable TV. Panic-stricken, we dashed through his living room.

"Hey, kids!" called Withers. "What's your hurry? How about a cup of hot chocolate?"

"Aaaaggghhhh!" we replied.

We heard him talk to the Trichophyton as they streaked after us in hot pursuit. "Well, golly, I guess you folks aren't from around here. Never mind. How about some hot chocolate?"

"Blaaghhraughharghhraablaahhh!" the Trichophyton replied.

I wish I could morph into a vegetable right now, I thought desperately. I couldn't even feel my burning lungs anymore. I was moving like a machine.

What vegetable would I be? I wondered. I tried to imagine it as I ran. Anything to drive away the horrible terror that had taken over my body. I couldn't afford to lose my head.

Maybe I'd be a head of lettuce! I thought.

And then I heard the Trichophytons' words in my brain. No—not in my brain, exactly. I heard their words through my feet, which were suddenly itching like crazy.

"Off with their heads!" called the fungus.

Chapter Nine

Just when I thought I was going to lose my head, Fun Gus called off the chase. "We'll get 'em later!" he shouted. "They're no threat to us!"

The fungi drew back, returning to Withers's field and their leader. We kept running, desperate to get as far away from that awful place as we could. Soon after, we split up, eager to return to the safety of our homes.

Later, I woke up in my own bed, drenched in sweat. "Wow, what a creepy dream," I said aloud.

Then I saw something in the corner of my room that made my heart stop beating and my hair stand straight up on my head.

"Don't be frightened," said the thing in the corner. "It's me. Cary. I did it. I morphed."

I blinked and rubbed my eyes. The thing was still there. I was looking at a giant carrot with arms and legs. I climbed slowly out of bed.

"How does it feel?" I whispered.

Now that I looked closely—really closely—I could tell Cary was in there somewhere. It wasn't obvious right away, but somehow I could see Cary's face—his eyes, nose, and mouth—toward the top of the giant carrot.

"It's strange—and . . . wonderful," said Cary. "There's an amazing calm that comes over you. I feel a little bit human, but stronger—crunchier, too. I can't describe to you what it's like to *feel like a color. To feel orange. To be a carrot.*"

I hope I wake up soon, I thought. I felt sick to my stomach.

"I can read your thoughts when you think so loudly," said Cary. "You've got to learn to think more quietly."

"Well, excuse me!" I snapped. "I'm just a little bit jumpy, okay? My friend turns up in my room as a six-foot-tall carrot. Hello!"

"Don't call me *carrot*," said Cary. "*Carrot* is the name for those unconscious, zombie lookalikes. I am *Daucus Carota*, a member of the Vegetable Kingdom and part of the family Umbelliferae."

"Pardon me." I couldn't resist being sarcastic. "I didn't know. You just looked like a big carrot to me. With arms and legs."

"Okay, okay. Relax," said Cary—I mean, Daucus Carota.

"I can't wait to communicate with some other members of my family, the Umbelliferae. They're probably living under Withers's field along with the other members of the Vegetable Kingdom."

I felt my friend's voice catch. "I'll have to pay my respects to Prince Brassica's family."

"Please let me wake up soon!" I said aloud.

"You aren't asleep!" the big carrot said. "Get that through your thick human skull. Now, watch what I can do."

Cary began to vibrate all over. Then he started to shrink. I stood still as a statue while Cary got smaller and smaller. His legs and arms disappeared inside his body. Then he jumped up on the dresser.

In seconds, you would never have known that there was anything more unusual than an ordinary carrot lying on my bureau. Except the ordinary-looking carrot could still talk to me.

"Do me a favor," he said. "There's something I would really like."

"What?" I asked. I couldn't believe that I hardly felt strange talking to a carrot.

"Go downstairs to the refrigerator and get some nice cool salad dressing and spread it on me like suntan lotion. It would really be great. And while you're down there, smell some of the vegetables deeply. You've got to try morphing. It's wonderful. I've never felt so alive as I am now as a vegetable."

Mega-weird, I thought.

"I don't know if I'm ready for this," I said. "Maybe we should call the police and let them know what's going on instead of playing around with being vegetables."

"Are you crazy?" Cary asked.

I took a deep breath. "I think maybe I am," I said.

41

"I was under a lot of pressure at school this year, you know. Now I'm talking to a carrot."

"Trust me," said Cary. "Just go get the salad dressing and take a couple of whiffs of some of the things in your vegetable bin. Don't knock it until you've tried it."

"Okay," I agreed. I felt like somebody had flicked a switch inside me and I was operating on automatic. I did as I was told.

Ever so quietly I crept downstairs to the kitchen. I opened the refrigerator door and peered into the vegetable bin. Through the clear plastic drawer I could see a tomato, a cucumber, some carrots, a bunch of radishes, an ear of corn, and a bunch of kale.

I slid the drawer out and grabbed the ear of corn. I inhaled deeply. Its odor was . . . fresh, yellow and green. I was inhaling the corn when my older brother came into the room.

"What in the world are you doing?" Bryce asked. His voice didn't sound right. It was raspy and hoarse. He didn't look good, either. He was pale.

"What's wrong with you?" I asked. I've always found that answering a question with a question is a good way to throw people off track.

"Sore throat," said Bryce. "Now, why are you sniffing an ear of corn?"

Great, I thought. My smooth diversionary tactic hadn't worked at all.

"I . . . uh, I've been trying to appreciate the small things in life more—the feeling of sunshine on my face, the taste of tapioca pudding, the smell of corn."

Bryce glared at me. "You're goofy," he said. "I don't believe you're standing there sniffing a vegetable. What a dork." Then he closed his eyes for a second. "I think I have a fever," he said softly. He turned to leave. "Sorry I snapped at you," he said.

I watched him go. I stared at the corn I was holding and thought, *I can't believe my ears.*

Calling me goofy and a dork wasn't surprising. That was business as usual. But I never, ever remembered Bryce apologizing to me.

Don't get me wrong—my brother and I got along okay. He just never went out of his way to demonstrate any brotherly affection. He wasn't the kind of brother who showed you how to throw a baseball or took you to your first movie. He was more the kind of brother who locked you in the closet when his friends came over and was always sneaking up behind you and yelling, trying to scare you half to death, Mom and Dad said it was because he liked me but just didn't know how to show it.

People thought Bryce was cool, though. Bryce was good-looking. He was captain of the football team and worked out at the gym all the time.

I guess Bryce has a really bad fever and sore throat, I thought. *That's why he doesn't seem like himself.* I sighed.

I picked up the ear of corn, grabbed a bottle of creamy Italian, and went up to my room.

"What took you so long?" asked Cary. "I feel like I've been waiting for about two hours."

I checked my watch. "Actually, you've been waiting for five minutes. I was talking to my brother." Then I

43

stopped dead in my tracks. "How long have you been a carrot?" I asked, my heart pounding in my chest.

"It seems like hours," said Cary.

"No!" I screamed. "Don't you remember what Prince Brassica said? *Never remain a vegetable longer than the recommended cooking time.* We still don't know what kind of cooking he was talking about, but hours is definitely too long for any vegetable."

"Yeah. I guess I kind of forgot," Cary said. He didn't sound too concerned.

"Look at the clock and check," I insisted. I picked up the carrot and took it over to the clock.

"Gee, I guess I was wrong. I've only been a vegetable for about fifteen minutes."

My thoughts were racing. He thought he'd been a vegetable for hours, but it was only minutes. He thought I'd been gone from the room for two hours, but it had been only five minutes. Maybe that meant that every five minutes in human time felt like hours in vegetable time.

Right now the most important thing was for Cary to get back into his human form. "Morph back, Cary!" I said. "Now!"

"Okay!" Cary agreed.

Just then the door to my room opened. It was Bryce.

"Who are you talking to, Kyle?" he asked.

"Uhh . . . nobody," I answered. My mind was reeling. Bryce was staring at me.

"I was rehearsing my lines for the community theater play," I said finally.

Bryce snorted. "Community theater play . . ." he echoed. "That's dumb."

"Uh, yeah," I said. I just wanted him to get out of there so Cary could morph back and didn't have to be a carrot forever.

Then Bryce saw the bottle of salad dressing on my bureau. "You know you're not supposed to eat in your room," he said. "What are you doing, making a salad up here? Yuck. We'll get bugs."

As I stood there speechless, Bryce grabbed the carrot and the salad dressing. "I'm putting this stuff back in the refrigerator. But then I want to talk to you."

The time was ticking away. I watched the digital clock on my night stand click from eight-fifteen to eight-sixteen.

"Let's talk later," I said. "Right now, I need to rehearse. So I need the salad dressing back. And the carrot. Please, Bryce."

Still holding Cary and the dressing, Bryce crossed his arms. "What's this play about, exactly?"

"It's . . . a comedy," I stammered. "Vegetables take over the world. You've heard of the movie *Attack of the Killer Tomatoes*, right? Well, this is kind of like that. I play an ear of corn."

Bryce's eyes narrowed. "Really? I've heard of the movie, but I didn't know there was a play."

I shrugged and tried not to look guilty. It was tough to lie to my brother. Usually I didn't dare.

Suddenly Bryce's face lit up with a smile. "Okay, kid," he said, ruffling my hair. "Listen, maybe I'll take

45

you to the movies or we can watch a video later. After I get back from working at Farmer Withers's."

"Sure," I said as soon as I was able to talk.

Bryce picked up the carrot. "But you're going to have to practice your lines without this," he said. "It doesn't belong in your room."

I followed Bryce downstairs and watched helplessly as he threw Cary in the vegetable bin and closed the refrigerator door.

Chapter Ten

Bryce crossed his arms and leaned against the refrigerator. "I feel so sick," he said. He sounded worse than before. "Maybe I have the flu."

Bryce doubled over and started to giggle. Then he straightened up and started dancing around the room, flapping his arms like wings. "I can flew, I can flew, because I've got the flu. Get it?"

Really lame, I thought. Aloud I said, "Um, yeah. *Flew* and *flu* . . . that's really funny."

"See you later, and maybe we'll watch a video together. Maybe a cartoon."

"Cartoon?" I echoed in disbelief.

"Yeah." Bryce giggled a little again. Then he said, "I've got to get back to Farmer Withers's place. I went by there at the crack of dawn, and I just had to come back for some aspirin. That guy doesn't know the meaning of the word *sick* when it's connected to the word *work*. He figures people should get sick only on their days off."

"Sure. You're absolutely right, Bryce." The words practically exploded out of my mouth. All I could think about was Cary lying there next to a bunch of supermarket vegetables and imagining never being human again.

Bryce smiled. "I don't know why he bothers with that field anyway. It sure would be great to see his face the day something finally grows there. If it ever does, I mean." He giggled again, then headed for the front door.

Beads of sweat were standing out on my forehead. I was reaching for the refrigerator door when the phone rang.

Bryce answered. "Kyle, it's for you," he called. "It's Tommy."

"I'll call him back," I shouted, my hand on the refrigerator. *Get out of here already, Bryce!* I thought.

I heard my brother stomp down the hall. The front door creaked as he opened it, then slammed shut.

I jerked the refrigerator open and pulled out the vegetable bin. I was afraid to look at the clock.

"Morph, carrot—I mean, Cary! Morph!" I said desperately to the carrot I had picked up.

Tick, tick, tick. Nothing happened. I was still holding a carrot.

"Morph!" I commanded the carrot. Then I heard a voice.

"Down here!"

Cary was still in the vegetable bin. I had been holding an ordinary carrot. I threw it back and pulled Cary out.

"I'm trying to morph, but I'm cold. Try holding me under some warm water. Quick! I can feel my body starting to change."

I turned on the hot water full blast and held Cary under the tap. I could feel him starting to vibrate. "Hey! Get me out from under here! I'm burning up!" he cried.

I pulled Cary out, put him on the counter, and turned off the water. *Please be all right, Cary*, I prayed silently.

The carrot continued to vibrate. The vibrations grew stronger and stronger. The carrot began to pulsate. Then there was some kind of little explosion, like the *pop!* of a balloon. The human Cary sat on the counter. He was naked and soaking wet.

At that moment, I heard the front door creak again. Then I heard Bryce's footsteps. They were coming toward the kitchen! I thought my nerves were going to jump right through my skin!

Quickly I pulled off my T-shirt. "Put this on!" I told Cary. Then I laid a dish towel over his lap. I stuck my head under the faucet and soaked my hair.

"Kyle, I forgot—hey, what's going on here?" Bryce said. "Cary, when did you get here—and why are you guys all wet?"

"It's a hot day. I just got here, and boy, I sweated up a storm coming over here. Kyle decided to cool off, too," Cary lied.

Pretty smooth, I thought with admiration.

"Well, we have a thing called air conditioning," Bryce said. Then he shrugged. "Kids. Enjoy yourselves. I just forgot to take some more aspirin with me. I may need it later if I still don't feel well. See you. I've got to go help the most unsuccessful farmer alive."

We both realized we'd been holding our breath when Bryce closed the door behind him. I let out an explosion of air and then inhaled deeply.

"That was too much for me. Between you and Bryce—" Suddenly my legs felt like jelly. I sat down on the kitchen floor. Cary sat down beside me.

"That was a close one," he said.

"You're not kidding," I told him. "You had about ten seconds to spare before you became part of tonight's salad."

"You wouldn't have let that happen."

"No," I assured him. "But then again, I picked the wrong carrot at first when I thought I was pulling you out of the vegetable bin."

Cary patted me on the shoulder. "You wouldn't have taken any chances. If you'd had to, you would have pulled *all* of the carrots out just to be sure." He tilted his head to one side. "That's why you've got to be the leader when we fight the Jerkks."

My head almost swiveled around on my neck. "Me? You must be kidding. I've always tried to think of myself as a leader, but these past couple of days, I've had to be honest with myself. People listen to you, but nobody listens to me. Not Tommy, or Randi, or Olivia, or my brother. Not anybody."

50

"That will change when . . ." Cary let his voice trail off.

I leaned forward. "When what?" I asked.

Cary got one of those faraway looks in his eye. "You know, I think maybe I wouldn't have minded remaining a carrot. As long as I didn't wind up as part of somebody's salad." He smiled.

"Come on, Kyle, let's get upstairs so I can get dressed, and you can try morphing." Cary stood up and began walking toward the stairs. I picked up the ear of corn and followed him.

Chapter Eleven

When we got to my room, Cary looked at me seriously. "I heard your brother talking when I was in the vegetable bin. Carrots have heightened senses, both hearing and seeing," he explained.

"Yeah, he was acting weird," I said. "He was sort of nice to me. Not like Bryce at all."

"He wasn't just acting weird," Cary said. "Think about it, Kyle—the way your brother was giggling and made that stupid joke about *flew* and *flu*."

"You didn't catch him dancing around the room while he said it. That was like . . . being in a science fiction movie, it was so strange."

Cary shook his head. "I don't think he was just acting weird or strange. I think your brother was acting like a *Jerkk*."

I gasped and collapsed onto the bed. I could feel the blood rushing through my brain. "You're right," I said when I finally could talk. "But we can't be sure the Jerkks got to him. Maybe he really is just sick."

"Maybe. But we've got to keep our eyes on him."

"Potatoes have lots of eyes, don't they? Maybe we should be potatoes," I tried joking.

Cary laughed slightly. "Okay, it's a little bit funnier than your brother's joke. But if you keep saying things like that, you're going to start worrying me."

"Look, I know it was dumb. I was only fooling around."

"In other words, you're not an airhead, you're a lettuce head," Cary joked back.

"That was *really* bad," I groaned, but I smiled. Just then the phone rang. I answered it and heard Farmer Withers's nasal twang on the other end of the line. But he sounded hoarse, too.

"Where the heck's your brother? He's supposed to be working," Farmer Withers demanded.

I held the receiver away from my ear and gaped at it. My brother was usually snotty, and suddenly he was being nice. And he was sick.

Farmer Withers was usually nice, even if he was kind of dotty in the head sometimes. Now he was being nasty. And he was sick.

I put the phone back to my ear and spoke into the mouthpiece. "He's on the way over. You sound sick, Farmer Withers."

"Mind your own business," he said. Then he added, "Oh, all right. I thought I had the flu." He giggled the same insane way my brother had. "Maybe I flew over the cuckoo's nest instead. I sure do feel cuckoo." He imitated some cuckoo-clock sounds and then hee-hawed.

"Anyway, I was wrong," he went on. "I called that quack doctor, Doc Smoot. He came over here and took a gander at me. Turns out I've got what they call strep throat. But I've never been happier in my life."

He's flipped, I thought. *Or maybe he's a Jerkk.* "Why are you so happy if you've got a strep throat?" I asked. I glanced at Cary and saw his eyes were wide.

"Because there's stuff growing all over my field! Mushrooms! It's a miracle! I can sell 'em to supermarket chains and soup companies!" he practically shouted into my ear.

"Ah, here comes your brother now." Farmer Withers hung up the phone with a slam and without so much as a *good-bye.* Usually he said, "Have a nice day. Take care of yourself. Best of luck. You need anything, just give a holler. Don't make yourself a stranger. You're always welcome to stop by for some hot chocolate. Well, 'bye now." It took him about five minutes just to get off the phone. And now—*bang!*

"I think Farmer Withers may be a Jerkk. He's got strep throat. That comes from a bacteria called streptococcus." I knew that stuff because my parents are doctors. They're both dermatologists. That means they specialize in skin diseases, but they know other medical stuff, too.

"Hmm. I've got a solid hunch that the strep has something to do with the fungi," said Cary. "I'm not

54

sure what, but I bet we'll find out soon enough."

"I think my brother's got it, too." I gulped as I thought about Bryce being sick. "He's been in Farmer Withers's field—which is now full of mushrooms, by the way. I'm pretty sure strep throat is contagious," I told him. "We'd better all get morphing soon. And I'll ask my mom and dad about this, too."

Cary was busy pulling on a pair of my pants. "We're going to have to figure out what to do about clothes," he said as he grabbed a T-shirt. "I'll wash these and get them back to you pronto. But we can't risk morphing back into humans and being left without anything on. I can't believe I was so excited about morphing that I forgot all about clothes."

"Yeah. Lock the door. I don't want to chance my parents arriving home and being surprised by a big ear of corn in my room."

"Okay." Cary walked over and locked my door. "Inhale the corn again, and then let yourself go. Let yourself *be* an ear of corn."

It was hard to imagine what he meant, but I knew I had to give it a try. So I held the ear to my nose and sniffed. At first, nothing happened. I started to think it wasn't going to work.

"I'm concentrating as hard as I can," I told Cary.

"Stop concentrating so hard and go with the flow," he said.

So I just stood there holding the ear of corn and waiting for something to happen. Then it did.

The feeling was incredible. I felt energy shoot

through me as suddenly I was supercharged with vitamin C and niacin. I could feel vitamin A, riboflavin, and thiamine surging through my veins, too.

My body started changing. My arms turned skinny and green while the rest of me changed into corn kernels. The last thing that happened was that my hair turned to corn silk, and I developed tough green leaves on my back.

"I feel pretty good," I told Cary. "And now I know why they're called ears of corn. My hearing has never been so clear. I can hear the little kids chanting while they jump rope next door." I started repeating their rhyme:

> "My back is achin',
> My belt's too tight,
> My feet are shakin'
> From left to right.
> Sound off!
> One, two!
> Sound off!
> Three, four!
> Let's all hear it
> Once more!"

"Let's not hear it once more. You're getting all fired up," said Cary. "Calm down. We've got some thinking to do."

Cary's words carried me back to reality—and fast. "You'd better believe it," I said. I checked the clock on

56

my night stand. Sure enough, only five minutes had gone by, but it felt like at least an hour in vegetable time.

Then I looked down at my jeans and shirt on the floor. "We've got to figure out what to do about *clothes*."

"Maybe Prince Brassica would have had ideas," Cary said sadly.

I let out a sigh. Just then the phone jangled. I heard the ringing so clearly that I jumped. Then I answered. "Hello?"

Before I heard the voice on the other end of the line, I caught a glimpse of myself in the mirror. A big, talking ear of corn holding a telephone. At first, the sight shocked me, but then it seemed perfectly normal. If you've never been an ear of corn, I guess that's hard to understand. You'll just have to take my word for it.

"Hello," replied a proud, deep voice. "This is Prince Brassica Oleracea Italica Cruciferae."

He was alive!

Chapter Twelve

That night at dinner, my mind kept drifting back to my conversation with Prince Brassica on the phone. What great news that he was still alive! He'd told me that he had crawled into the vegetable tunnel and hidden himself. That's how he had survived. His friends and family had nursed him back to health.

My father's voice broke into my thoughts. "Eat your vegetables," he said.

"You know how important that is," my mother chimed in. "Not one of you has touched your salad."

Bryce gave my friends and me a narrow look of suspicion. Randi, Olivia, Tommy, and Cary had come over for dinner. We planned to practice morphing afterward.

My mother had made crab cakes along with salad and two vegetables. It must have been fate that made her choose broccoli and corn. There were carrot curls in the salad. All my friends and I had been able to eat was the crab cakes and bread and butter. It was tough enough to eat at all, staring at things that reminded us of Prince Brassica and other members of the Vegetable Kingdom.

"Why is everybody suddenly allergic to vegetables?" Bryce spoke up. My father had given him some antibiotics, and they must have worked wonders because he looked and sounded much better.

But I knew from my conversation with Prince Brassica that antibiotics would only make things worse in the long run. Our broccoli friend had clued me in to a lot of facts—the clothes thing for one.

He told us we could morph our clothes into invisibility and back again. We still had to try it. As far as I was concerned, I wasn't going to morph outside the house until I had that skill down pat. Morphing *inside* the house was risky enough.

Now back to the antibiotics. Prince Brassica was pretty sure that the attack of the Streptococcus soldiers was a trick—a decoy.

Apparently antibiotics can kill the Streptococcus soldiers, but using them can leave a person more vulnerable to invasion by fungus. It would make it easier for the next level of Jerkks, the Trichophyton, to get hold of their victims.

There would probably be an epidemic of athlete's foot. Of course, it wouldn't be ordinary athlete's foot. It would be *super* athlete's foot.

I didn't have to ask my parents how to treat athlete's

foot, because Prince Brassica had already told me. There were antifungal creams available in drugstores. What they did was engulf the fungus—the fancy word for it was *phagocytosing*, which I thought was interesting but too long and hard to pronounce. I just thought of it as the good guys destroying the bad guys.

However, Prince Brassica said the creams might not work on the mutated super athlete's foot fungus, and even if they did, the Trichophyton could just infect their victims again. The soldiers needed to be stamped out and kept from infecting feet permanently. That's where we came in—by helping the Vegetable Kingdom kill the soldiers with massive charges of vitamins and minerals.

"Stop daydreaming and eat," my father told me.

"Eat those vegetables," said my mom.

I took a deep breath and looked down at my plate. *These aren't really members of the Vegetable Kingdom*, I told myself. They hadn't talked to me from the vegetable bin that day. They were just mindless lookalikes.

I swallowed hard and took a bite of broccoli. After the first bite, it wasn't so difficult. I speared a tomato and chewed.

For once, I *was* the leader of the group. The rest of my friends started eating their vegetables. Bryce kept staring at us for a while and then ate his.

I managed to choke down most of mine. I just kept telling myself that I was doing it for Prince Brassica and the rest of the Vegetable Kingdom. One thing I could do to help them was not let anyone suspect that my friends and I were their allies.

"May we be excused now?" I asked when my plate was practically empty. Randi, Olivia, Cary, and Tommy had rallied, too.

"Fine," said my mom. "What are you all planning to do?"

"Um—go downstairs to the rec room and work on a school project together," I managed to lie. I hate lying, and I'm not very good at it. But for now I had no choice.

"Glad to hear you're getting serious about school," said Dad. That's what he always said. I got pretty good grades. I think it's just something his dad said to him, so he passed it on.

I could feel Bryce's eyes on us as we left the table. "Schoolwork in the summertime? I thought we were going to watch cartoons together," he said.

"We want to get a jump on the fall semester," I told him. Mom and Dad cracked up. "Glad to hear you're developing a sense of humor, son," said Dad.

My four friends and I hurried downstairs to the basement recreation room. I had already hidden some vegetables under the foldout couch down there.

I pulled out the paper bag. "What do you guys want to be?" I asked. I held out a carrot, a tomato, a jar of olives, a radish, and a bunch of kale. "I couldn't take too much bulky stuff, or my parents might notice it missing from the vegetable bin. I'd like to try the kale myself, since it's kind of like my name. This afternoon I was an ear of corn. I think my mom cooked the one I used to morph for dinner."

Randi scrunched down on her knees and picked up

each one of the vegetables. "I was a giant lima bean today," she said. "It was the strangest feeling. Strong, but calm. I felt green. A pale green. I never thought you could *feel* like a color before."

"I know exactly what you're talking about," I told her.

"Me, too," said Cary. "If no one minds, I'd like to be the carrot again. When I was one earlier today, it just felt right to me."

Randi tilted the striped cap she was wearing, shrugged, and handed Cary the carrot. "Okay by me," she said.

"Okay," the rest of us said in unison.

A look of peace came over Cary's face when he held the carrot. An uncomfortable feeling stirred in my stomach. I didn't know why. I pushed the feeling aside.

"I'll take the olives," Olivia said next. "They seem like an interesting choice. Besides, olives are like *my* name."

Tommy tossed the tomato in the air. "This would have been my first choice anyway. I'll be Tommy Tomato."

As Randi grabbed the radish, I took a deep breath. "Let's get started. Remember what I told you about morphing the clothes?"

"Sure," said Randi. "You have to think of being the vegetable and of making the clothes invisible, one thought after the other, again and again while you inhale the vegetable."

"Right." I nodded. "Okay, everybody. Let's do it." I

closed my eyes and inhaled the leafy kale. Morphing into a vegetable was easier this time, but making the clothes invisible was tough for me.

It seemed to be a snap for everybody else. When we were finished morphing, I was looking at a plain carrot, tomato, radish, and olive. I was a bunch of kale, all right, but although my shirt was invisible, I still could see my jeans and one sneaker.

"Whoops! Check out Kyle, everybody. The first kale wearing a pair of jeans and a sneaker."

For some reason, everyone found this hilarious. I didn't. I could feel myself blushing right down to the bottom of my green leaves. "Very funny. Thanks for being such great friends," I said sourly.

"Don't take it so seriously, Kyle. We aren't trying to be mean. Just give it another go. You can do it," Cary encouraged me. The others cheered me on, too.

"Go for it, Kyle!" said Tommy.

"Don't give up!" urged Olivia.

"Yeah! Yeah!" said Randi and Cary.

I revved myself up. *You can do this, you can do this*, I repeated silently. Then I tried again. I thought, *Kale-invisible-kale-invisible*, chanting it over and over in my mind.

It worked. I looked at my body and saw only dark green leaves and skinny, stalklike green arms and legs.

"Yes!" said my friends all at once. I looked at Olivia, and she looked gorgeous to me as an olive. She was such a bright, shiny green.

In fact, everyone looked great to me as vegetables. In

some way, it felt like they were the same as my human friends, only . . . more. Everything was different. I felt so strong and deep green. At that moment, I knew that if a carrot was the right vegetable for Cary, then kale was right for me.

There was a knock at the door, and I heard Bryce's voice. "Hey, okay if I come down, you guys? I want to get a video."

I froze. We all froze. In fact, I actually saw frost on my leaves. Icicles dripped from the tomato. Little bits of ice crystals had formed on the carrot, the olive, and the radish.

We all stood there—like a bunch of frozen vegetables. Then we heard Bryce turning the doorknob.

"Okay, have it your way and don't answer me. I'm coming down right now."

The door began to creak as it opened.

Chapter Thirteen

Morph! *Morph! Morph!* I screamed in my brain. I had never been so terrified in all my life. I could tell that my friends felt the same way.

I began to sweat in fear. I could feel myself heating up, defrosting. I heard Bryce's heavy footsteps on the stairs.

Then it was as if something took over, and a wonderful calmness and clarity overcame me. I morphed. And luckily, I ended up with all my clothes on.

Somehow my friends all morphed, too. It seemed that it took forever, but I remembered that vegetable time was different from human time.

The instant Bryce showed his face, we were all back to normal—well, as normal as could be expected. After all, changing into a vegetable and back again in barely a minute isn't an experience most people go through. It gets you all tossed up inside, and it's not like tossing salad. That's fun. It's more like tossing your cookies.

"How come you're all just standing around?" Bryce asked. He knitted his brows and frowned. Then, suddenly, his face brightened in a big un-Bryce-like smile. "Hey, bro, you and your friends want to watch a cartoon video?" he asked.

"We don't have cartoon videos anymore, Bryce. We got rid of them years ago, remember?"

Bryce frowned again. "Phooey. Videorama is closed by now. Why do we have to live in such a hick town?" he whined.

"Sorry you're disappointed," I said after a moment. I couldn't think of anything else to say.

Bryce rubbed his right foot over his left. Then he rubbed the left foot over his right. He did it again.

My mouth dropped open. I closed it quickly.

"Looks like you're doing some scratching," said Cary. "Itchy? Like, maybe you've got athlete's foot?"

"I don't know," Bryce answered sullenly. "I'm really bummed about the cartoon. I was looking forward to it." He turned his back and stomped away.

I felt a wave of relief wash over me as soon as I heard the basement door close. "Whew!" I gasped. "That was the closest call I've ever had." My heart was pounding and my knees felt weak.

"We did it, though," Olivia said quietly. "I feel stronger now."

"So do I," said Tommy.

Cary and Randi looked at me and nodded in agreement.

Suddenly, I felt stronger, too. "We've still got to practice morphing before we go up against the Jerkks," I said. "I don't feel safe about practicing here, either. Let's walk down to the field at the end of the street. There won't be anybody there, and nothing bad ever happens there."

"Nothing bad ever happened in this town, until now," said Randi.

"So we've got to stop it." Cary was firm. "We'll go out the back door, get down there, and practice morphing until we can do it in our sleep."

I scratched my head. My hair felt a little strange after having leaves. "I don't think I could ever morph in my sleep."

"It's just a figure of speech," Cary explained. "But you never know what's possible until you try."

"Okay, let's go down to that field. But be quiet. We've got to look out for Bryce. I don't know where he's lurking in the house. Mom and Dad are probably upstairs, but watch out for them, just in case."

More quiet than mice—as quiet as vegetables—we crept up the basement steps.

I peered cautiously into the hall. I could hear the sound of the TV coming from the living room. "I think maybe Bryce is watching cartoons on cable," I whispered. "Not grownup cartoons, either. The kind little kids watch."

I looked around the corner, and sure enough, there was Bryce. He started giggling crazily at the antics of a cartoon pig. He had his shoes off and kept reaching down to scratch his feet.

I held a finger to my lips, silently motioning *shhhh!* I waved everyone toward the kitchen. From there we could get out through the garage.

The others followed me. We were almost safely out when I heard a crash. I whirled around.

Tommy was wearing a horrified look on his face. At his feet was a potted plant that we kept on a stand next to a little window.

"Hey, what's that noise?" I heard Bryce shout. Then his footsteps came stomping toward us.

Chapter Fourteen

Once more, it looked as if our stalks were going to be cooked by Bryce. But we were saved by the bell. Literally. The front doorbell rang.

I could hear Bryce hesitate for a moment. Then he turned around to answer the door. It was Bryce's best friend, Norman Drinkwater.

Oops! Oh, no! I told you his last name. Now I've gone and spilled the lima beans—or the baked beans or whatever—and gotten us all in the soup.

Please, please don't tell anyone. I told you I couldn't keep a secret. And I'm not a good liar.

Hey, wait a minute. Hold on. I really had you going there, didn't I? Ha! Ha!

Listen, I was just kidding around. The guy's last name isn't Drinkwater at all. It's Drainwater. And his family's phone number is unlisted. So you could never find him. But don't tell anybody anyway, okay?

It's easy to see why Norman and Bryce are such good friends. They're so much alike. But I could tell that Norman had changed, and he had become just like Bryce all over again.

"Duh, do your feet itch a lot?" was the first question Norman asked. I could just imagine him shuffling into the house.

Norman is big for his age. He's big for anybody's age. He plays on the football team like Bryce. He's a linebacker, and he can stop any number of people on the opposing team cold. I'd bet trying to tackle Norman is like trying to wrestle with an eighteen-wheeler. And having *him* tackle *you* is probably like being run over by the same truck.

"Uh, yeah, but so what?" answered my brother. He wasn't hoarse at all anymore. He and Norman had the same kind of strange, flat tone to their voices. It was like their minds were on hold.

Their minds were on hold.

A little shudder went through me. I knew my brother and Norman were both becoming Jerkks. Jerkk slaves.

The TV pig squealed, and Bryce giggled. "Come on. I'm watching this great cartoon. It's really cool."

"Okay, dude," Norman answered.

I shuddered again. No matter what Bryce had put me through, he was still my brother. Somewhere inside his twisted brain, he cared for me. And I cared for him. But now his brain wasn't twisted anymore. It was growing blanker by the minute as the fungus grew on him.

I motioned my friends toward the door. The only

70

way to help Bryce was to get on with what we had to do: master morphing and help the Vegetable Kingdom until there were enough of them to help us.

Even after we had crept through the kitchen door and out through the garage, everyone was strangely quiet. "I know what you're all thinking," I said. "That my brother and his friend are both becoming Jerkks."

"Yeah. I'm sorry," said Cary.

"We can help stop it, though," said Olivia. But her voice wavered.

Soon we came to the end of the street. Across the road was an open field.

I'll never forget that night. It was twilight and the sky was full of stars. We all became Vegemorphs that night. And there were no more clothing problems. Cary, Tommy, Randi, Olivia, and I all morphed into vegetable after vegetable.

"I feel like I'm a salad!" Randi laughed joyously at one point.

"Mixed green, tomato 'n' onion, or Caesar?" asked Cary. He was laughing, too.

"*Beets* me!" Randi answered.

"If only the Jerkks would *lettuce* alone!" I cried, joining in the fun.

"Never mind, we'll figure out how to *squash* them," said Olivia.

"We're getting pretty *corny*," Tommy added. "And speaking of corn, I'm *popped*."

"You mean *pooped*," I said. "How could you possibly be tired?"

Tommy danced by me. "I just said it to a*maize* you," he replied. "Actually, I'm full of pep. In fact, I'm feeling *pepper* every minute."

So there we were: a bunch of happy, laughing vegetables dancing under the stars, tossed to and fro. I'll never forget it. I'd never felt so alive, so vegetable-juiced up as I did then. But it wasn't going to last long.

"I *yam* what I *yam*," said Randi, who had morphed into a sweet potato. It was then we heard the noise—rustling in the bushes.

A group of guys came toward us. A feeling of horror swept over me as I realized who it was: the Biff Bunch from the mall.

In the gentle glow of twilight, I could see that Biff and his boys all had nasty smiles. I knew without a doubt that they had seen everything.

There was no time to morph. "Run!" I yelled.

We all started racing across the field. At least, we tried. You see, we had mastered morphing, but we hadn't mastered moving fast as vegetables.

I wanted to run fast, as if I were in a salad spinner. Instead, my skinny purple legs couldn't balance my fat eggplant body, and I fell down. Randi, Olivia, and Tommy were having the same problems. Soon a big artichoke, a cabbage, and a sweet potato were on the ground, kicking and screaming.

Cary, who was a bunch of celery, almost stalked away. But soon he, too, fell down.

Biff and the boys were standing over us. "When I saw you guys, I went and got my salad fork," he said.

"We saw you before you turned into vegetables, and we know you're those dweebs who hang out at the bingo parlor. You'd better tell us how you turn into vegetables, or you'll end up in a blender."

I knew Biff would enjoy giving me a cauliflower ear. He and his bunch were like identical peas in a pod. We had to cooperate, but we couldn't let him *leek* the story. Our vegetable shapes might help us fight fungus, but they wouldn't keep us from being diced by Biff and his buddies. Besides, we couldn't remain vegetables for too much longer or we'd be stuck.

"We'd better morph back, guys," I said. My friends had started already. In seconds, we were back in our own bodies. We struggled to our feet and faced Biff and his pals, Bongo, Sid, Spike, and Rudy.

"I'll tell you how it's done, but you won't like it," I told Biff.

Biff doubled up his fists. "I'm pretty steamed," he said. "Start talking or I'll wok you."

"Okay, okay," I agreed hurriedly. "I have to think of a vegetable, and while I'm thinking of it, I have to tell you the most boring thing I can think of. Then you'll be able to morph into that vegetable. After that, you can become any vegetable you want."

"That's cool!" said Biff. His sidekicks all nodded, as they usually did whenever he said anything. Biff had an eager gleam in his eyes, and his face was flushed. He wasn't asking me any details, and that gave me an idea.

"Start out with celery stalks," Cary advised us. "They're easy to do and lots of fun. Just stay away from parties, or you might end up stuffed with cream cheese and walnuts."

"All right, all right," I said. "Give me a minute to think of something boring." I shifted from one foot to the other.

"It ought to be easy for a dweeb like you," Biff commented.

"Right." I nodded. "Now, listen closely. Here goes." I began to recite a recipe for oxtail soup. By the way, don't try this at home. I made it up on the spot as I went along. I'm sure it's terrible.

I took a deep breath and began to talk in a singsong voice:

> "Take a couple of ox tails.
> Add some raisins and some ketchup.
> Don't forget fudge frosting.
> And some vanilla goo.
> Then put the whole mess in a big pot.
> Add four quarts of water.
> Put the whole thing on the stove,
> And simmer for an hour or two."

By the time I had gotten that far, Biff and his buddies were wearing glazed expressions and turning green. When I got to the part about dishing out the soup, they had all turned into stalks of celery.

Chapter Fifteen

Cary caught my eye. He gave a meaningful look, but I had no idea what it meant. He began talking to Biff and his buddies.

"Now that you know how to change into vegetables, let me tell you why we morph. It's not just for fun." Cary quickly filled Biff and his friends in on how our town, our state, our country, and our entire planet—maybe even our whole galaxy—were in danger. When he finished, he looked at Biff and his group, who were all standing around as celery stalks, and asked them, "Will you help?"

Biff didn't miss a single *beet*. "Ha! You've got to be kidding—or crazy. The idea of the earth being taken over by fungus and helping a bunch of talking vegetables . . ." His voice trailed off, and he doubled over with laughter.

Cary looked at me and gave a slight shake of his

head. He mouthed the words *Don't tell.* He looked at the rest of our friends and did the same thing. They all nodded.

"I'd like to point out, Biff, that *you* are a giant talking stalk of celery. If that isn't crazy to you, why don't you believe my story? And why won't you help?"

Biff strutted his green self up to Cary. "Maybe I believe you and maybe I don't," he said. "It doesn't matter, because I wouldn't help you anyway."

Biff turned around and looked at Bongo, Spike, Sid, and Rudy. "You guys wouldn't help, either, would you?"

The green leaves on top of each of the four stalks swiveled from side to side—*no.*

Biff turned back to Cary and the rest of us. "There's your answer. We won't help you." Then he gave us the celery version of a smile. "I think maybe we can have lots of fun as vegetables." His smile grew wider.

"Imagine how easy it will be to shrink down and sneak into the movies. If someone tries to stop us, we'll start growing and talking and scare the living daylights out of them." He and his friends laughed.

Biff's smile widened. He brightened so much that he became a brilliant, glowing green. "Free vacations!" he shouted. "Simple to pop yourself into some carry-on luggage and arrive in Puerto Rico in a few hours. Then you can get a hotel room for free and spend a week or two tanning on the beach."

Suddenly Biff stopped talking. "Hey, wait a minute. A celery can't tan on the beach. It probably can't even swim. How do I get back to being human? Tell me right now."

Great, I thought. I had hoped that blockhead Biff wouldn't get around to figuring out that obvious question, but he did. I opened my mouth to speak, but Cary nudged me in the ribs and again mouthed, *Don't tell!*

I don't know what was the matter with me. The whole situation must have short-circuited my brain. It was obvious what Cary meant, but I just didn't get it. Duh.

"Don't tell what?" I asked as I rubbed my side where he had nudged me in the ribs.

Cary got right up in my face and yelled, "Cooking time!"

Clang! Clang! Clang! A bell went off in my head. A light bulb went off, too. Of course! What we had to do was not tell Biff about the cooking-time rule. That way he couldn't *leek* our story.

Biff was one furious celery stalk. "What's going on here? There better not be something you're not telling me." Now Biff was in my face. "Talk!" screamed the stalk.

"Let me explain . . ." Cary began. But Biff fairly blew up in an explosion of leafy green. "I don't want *you* to explain. I want *Kyle* to explain."

My heart sank to the bottom of my hightops. Like I said, I'm no good at lying, and I don't like it. But if there ever was a good reason to lie, I had one now. The fate of everyone on Earth was in my hands.

"N-no, Biff, we're not keeping anything important from you," I stammered. "All you have to do to become human again is to think about being human while you recite the most boring thing you can think of. Like the recipe for Jell-O."

"What is the recipe for Jell-O?" Biff asked nastily.

"Just follow the package directions," I replied as coolly as I could.

For once in his life, Biff looked unsure of himself. I was staring at a once confident, but now insecure celery stalk. "What's the story with the cooking time?"

I looked him right in his beady green eyes. "Cooking time . . . it's time for our cookout. It's going to be just the five of us, because . . . because—"

"Because it's Olivia's birthday," Randi finished for me. "We're having a little celebration. It's not that we don't like you, even though you're always pelting us with apple cores. It's just that—well, you know how it is when you just want to get together with your best buds. We've got to get over to Barbecue Barn before it closes to pick up the hot dogs and rolls."

"Okay, Randi." Biff sounded suddenly shy. "You know, I've always thought you were kind of cute."

Randi looked like she was turning as green as a celery stalk. I was afraid she was going to get sick, but she didn't. Somehow she managed to flash Biff a big smile.

"Thanks, Biff," she said. "Maybe I'll see you later. Why don't you and your friends head over to Veggie Village? They've got a great salad bar. I'm sure you'll all meet some hot tomatoes there."

She and Cary looked at each other and winked. I still didn't quite get it, and I didn't find out what their plan was until a few days after our encounter with the Biff Bunch.

Chapter Sixteen

A couple of days later the five of us were spending the afternoon hanging out at the greenhouse Olivia's mom and dad owned. We were wondering when Prince Brassica would contact us next. We were all getting really nervous. Nobody was getting strep throat anymore, but now there was an epidemic of athlete's foot in town. None of us even got in the shower without shower clogs on.

The drugstores were all sold out of antifungal creams and pills. My parents were going nuts working overtime. Even though they worked late every night, their offices were still so overloaded with patients that they had to buy folding chairs and set them up in rows in the waiting rooms.

"I've never seen anything like it," my father had said that morning. "I think this is some kind of new, resistant strain of fungus, and it's spreading faster than whipped butter on burned toast."

"I think we'd better get some samples to the Centers for Disease Control," Mom had said. Both my parents looked drawn and tired.

Cary, Randi, Olivia, Tommy, and I were getting lots of suspicious looks, too. "How come you're not scratching?" people of all ages would stop us on the street and ask us. "How come you don't have *it*—the athlete's foot?"

"I tell them I never take my shoes off," said Randi. "I like to see them stare."

"It's not funny," Cary replied. He had morphed into a carrot. He was doing it more and more these days. Nobody talked about it. It was like some kind of unwritten rule. But I knew we were all thinking the same thing: that Cary seemed to prefer being a vegetable to being a person.

"It's weird," Olivia commented. "I've always talked to plants. It's supposed to help them thrive, and some people think that they can understand you. But I never thought of talking to vegetables."

I raked my fingers through my hair. "Well, good. Apparently you don't need to talk to the ones that don't talk back to you. That's why it's okay to eat them. Otherwise, I'd feel like a cannibal."

Randi tilted her hat back. It was straw and trimmed with red chili peppers. "I don't feel like a cannibal," she said. "As long as the vegetables don't talk and they're not the super vegetables of the Vegetable Kingdom," she added. Then she stood up.

"I'm hungry," she said. "Anybody else ready for lunch?"

Right on cue, my stomach growled. "I'm in," I agreed.

The whole bunch of us headed down to Main Street. There aren't many towns like the one where we live. I guess I shouldn't have told you that. But you already know how much trouble I have keeping secrets. I guess it's not a big clue anyway.

Main Street in our town is just what it says. The main street. No other streets have anything important. For that, you've got to go out to the mall.

Maybe I didn't mention it, but our mall isn't a very big one like those you'd see in Seattle, Washington, or Berkeley, California.

I guess I just gave you another clue. Well, that's not much of one, either. So now you know we don't live in Seattle or Berkeley.

Anyway, Main Street is a mixture of businesses that have been there for years, run mostly by nice old geezers like Sammy Spogue, who owns Spogue's Hardware. They actually still scoop nails out of big barrels at Spogue's. But I'm getting off the track.

There are a few new stores and restaurants that look wildly out of place. I saw Olivia reach for the door handle of one of them.

"Wait a minute," I said. "You never wanted to go to Veggie Village before. I don't like the feeling I'm getting."

"Get over it, Kyle," said Tommy. "They have great pita pockets, and you can make your own."

"I know," I answered. A knot twisted uncomfortably in my stomach, but I followed the others in.

I headed over to the counter, but Randi called out to me. "Hey, Kyle, come over here to the salad bar."

"Nah . . . I think I'll just get a tofu burger," I said.

Randi laughed. So did Olivia, Cary, and Tommy. "You're chicken."

"I've never been a chicken, but I've been a vegetable," I reminded her.

"You know very well what I mean," said Randi. "We all planned this." I saw her look into a tray of celery stalks and then glance at me. "Here's why you couldn't tell the Biff Bunch about the cooking time." She peered back into the celery tray. "Is that you, Biff?" she asked. "Sid? Bongo? Spike?"

I was getting more uncomfortable by the minute. People were turning to stare at us.

I walked over to Randi and the others. "Cut it out," I said. "We look really weird. Besides, what if one of these celery stalks is one of those guys?" The thought really grossed me out.

"Kyle, stop it," said Olivia. "You know it's okay to eat vegetables that don't talk back." Now the whole bunch of them started staring into the celery tray and calling out the names of the Biff Bunch.

"Sid? This one looks like you. You always had that unhealthy, wilted look."

"Rudy? Talk to me, dude."

"Spike? Are you in there? Say something."

"Biff? Who's the big guy now?"

A hush fell over the restaurant. People who were eating stopped chewing. They stopped with their forks in midair. The staff behind the counter wearing vegetable hats stared.

Finally I caught on completely. "If Biff and his buddies can't morph back, they can't tell anyone about *us*. They don't know enough about morphing to talk to people." I scowled at my friends. "Why wouldn't you explain it to me before?"

"We thought you'd be able to figure it out," said Cary.

Then we heard a voice coming from the other end of the salad bar.

"Pssst! Get over here!"

Now my five friends and I stared at each other. We weren't laughing and joking anymore. We heard the voice again.

"Pssst! It's me, Prince Brassica Oleracea Italica Cruciferae. I'm over here in the broccoli tray with my whole family. We've been waiting to talk to you."

A middle-aged woman with a bouffant hairdo and a Hawaiian shirt walked over to the salad bar. She bent down close to the broccoli tray. "Did you just say something?" she asked.

Prince Brassica stood straight up in the tray and said in a deep green voice, "*Beet* it, lady. We've got important business to talk about."

The woman turned deathly pale. She shrieked. Then everybody else in the restaurant screamed and ran for the door.

Chapter Seventeen

The wild scene at Veggie Village was horrible and hilarious at the same time. Prince Brassica and his family kept getting taller by the second.

People looked over their shoulders as they ran. They couldn't believe their eyes. They couldn't believe their ears, either, because Prince Brassica was talking. He was ordering everyone around as if they were members of his Vegetable Kingdom. With his skinny, tentacle-like arms on his hips, he was shouting:

"Calm down, everyone! You're acting like a bunch of frightened baby green peas!" His words didn't do anything to calm anyone down, however. In fact, the talking broccoli stalk just made everyone more hysterical.

Spoons, forks, napkins, and plates full of the daily vegetarian special flew into the air as people hurried to get out of the place. I got hit in the nose with a spoonful of garlic vinaigrette. It burned a little.

"Form a single line! Proceed to the exit in an orderly fashion!" thundered Prince Brassica.

"Eeeeekkk!" screeched a woman with big hair as she raced by. "It's the attack of the killer broccoli! We're all going to get creamed!"

A little boy pointed his toy laser gun at the prince. "Zap! Zap! Zap! You vegetable space alien!" he cried.

A man broke a window and climbed through it. Then the crowd broke the door down.

It was horrible to see all these nice people acting so crazy. *If they only knew what they* really *have to fear*, I thought. They were all afraid of the *good guys*.

Soon Prince Brassica, his family, my friends, and I were the only ones in the restaurant. There were no customers left, and no staff. The walls were splattered with all kinds of salad dressing: Thousand Island, creamy Italian, garlic vinaigrette—you name it.

"This is cool," said one of Prince Brassica's kids. She smeared a glob of dressing all over herself.

"Stop that," Prince Brassica said sternly.

"I'm taking the kids home. They've had too much excitement," said mama broccoli. She and the children suddenly shrank in size. They skittered outside and disappeared down a storm drain.

"They're taking a shortcut home," Prince Brassica explained. He pulled out a chair. As he sat down, he motioned for my friends and me to take a seat at the table with him.

"I don't think we should sit by the window," I said quietly. "It might scare the people walking by."

Prince Brassica nodded. "You're right. Let's go back and talk in the kitchen."

So we all trooped into the restaurant's kitchen and sat among the pots and pans. We waited with eager anticipation to hear what Prince Brassica would say.

He leaned toward us. "It's nearly time to strike. We can't wait any longer."

"Just a moment." I couldn't stop myself from interrupting. "We've been waiting for you to contact us. How did you know we'd come into Veggie Village today?"

A mysterious smile swept over Prince Brassica's face. "Let's just call it vegetable intuition," he said. "You may be able to develop it after morphing for quite a while. On the other hand, you may not. Only time will tell. Right now we have to talk about attack strategy."

I wanted to know more about vegetable intuition, but I didn't ask. I realized our situation had gone from bad to worse.

Practically everybody in town was scratching like mad, and they didn't seem to care anymore. My brother had stopped using his antifungal cream, and his athlete's foot looked terrible. It was all red and scaly. Plus he'd developed a rash on his back.

"My brother is acting really strange," I told Prince Brassica. I got up from the counter and began pacing back and forth. "Like everybody else in town, he doesn't seem to mind his gross athlete's foot and the rash on his back. He's stopped treating it. And another thing, he's been trying to get me to go to these meetings called the Snorings."

"I've heard about those things," said Cary. "People have a party in the mushroom field at Farmer Withers's place. They all bring sleeping bags and stay overnight. After that, each camper has a rash the next day. We've got to do something fast!"

"You bet your sweet potato we do," said Prince Brassica.

"But how can we do anything if nobody cares that they're infected?" I asked.

"Stop interrupting and let me explain!" the prince snapped.

Wow. He was touchy today. I shut up and sat down.

"At the Snorings, people eat a lot of mushroom soup. That starts the infection. But tomorrow night, another fungus is going to get them: the Rubrum Jerkks. They won't be happy about that."

We all had the same question for Prince Brassica. *What happened when the Rubrum Jerkks got you?*

"The Rubrum are the worst Jerkks of all. And these are mutants, which makes them even more dangerous. Even ordinary Rubrum fungus will turn your nails a yucky, slimy yellow and green."

I looked down at my hands. My friends did the same. I felt sick at the thought of my nails getting covered with fungus.

"The worst thing about Rubrum is that it's so hard to get rid of. Even the ordinary Rubrum is tough to treat with regular antifungal cream. It can take years. Once this mutant variety gets hold of you, I don't know how long it could last. And it attacks vegetables, too."

I sucked in my breath. "What are we going to do?" I blurted.

Prince Brassica glared at me. "I told you, no interruptions!" He folded his tentacled arms over his chest. "We've got to use a combination of antifungal cream and a healthy zap of vegetable vitamins and minerals. That will get rid of them for good."

I remembered how Prince Brassica had zapped the Trichophyton soldiers that first night. But I hadn't the faintest notion of how to do it.

The prince must have had another attack of vegetable intuition, because he answered the question as if he had read my mind.

"You'll have no problem zapping. Once you've learned to morph, the knowledge is part of your roots. Just point one tentacled finger and think *zap!* That's all there is to it.

"Listen carefully," Prince Brassica went on. "You've got to squirt everyone with antifungal cream and then zap them. You've got to do the same to every fungus you meet."

Now we were hanging on his every word. I felt hypnotized.

"We're going to have to hijack some truckloads of antifungal cream from that pharmaceutical supply place just outside of town," the royal broccoli said. "You'll smear some on yourselves before you morph. And be careful. Don't let anyone at the Snoring think

88

you're anything but ordinary vegetables. Just lay low and wait for your chance."

"What about bacteria?" I blurted. I just couldn't help myself.

"I'm getting to that," Prince Brassica replied. "We're not going to kill the bacteria. They're weakened already. Besides, killing bacteria could make the fungus stronger."

The prince put his broccoli face close to mine. "If any bacteria bother you"—he waved a green fist in the air—"just *wok* 'em!"

Chapter Eighteen

"**G**oing to the Snoring tonight, anyone? Or is it just me?" asked my brother the following evening at dinner. He looked me right in the eyes in an almost threatening way as he said it.

"Your dad and I are very interested in these Snorings we've been hearing about," said my mother. "But you know, we're just so busy all the time treating these strange rashes." She took a sip of water.

"Now it's even harder to treat people, because they don't bother to come in," she went on. "But if they don't, the rashes will get worse and worse."

"I just don't understand it," my father said. "If I had these rashes and awful, scaly athlete's foot, I'd want to get rid of them right away."

"Maybe the situation isn't as bad as you think," my brother said in a low voice. "Maybe it's a good thing."

"Oh, Bryce, you're making those strange jokes of

yours again," Mom said. "I thought you were beginning to lighten up, but there you go again."

"You've been acting like some creature in a bad science fiction movie lately." My father frowned.

Bryce ignored their remarks. He looked at me. "So how about you? You and your friends don't have athlete's foot or rashes. What's keeping you from coming to a Snoring?"

I poked at the vegetables on my plate and tried not to look guilty. Inside I was a nervous wreck about the coming night.

"Oh, maybe we'll all stop by," I lied. I hoped I was getting better at it.

"Why don't you come with me when I drive over?" Bryce asked. I could tell he was testing me—pushing, watching my reaction.

"I guess I could . . . but I've gotten so deep into this book I'm reading. I'll probably walk over later with Tommy and the rest of the gang."

"What's the book you're reading?" Bryce demanded. He just wasn't going to give up. And I was floundering.

Luckily, I was saved by my dad. "That's enough, Bryce. Reading is good for you. Leave your brother alone and go to the Snoring by yourself. I think he's too young to stay out all night with anything but a scout troop anyhow."

I almost jumped out of my chair and hugged my dad. For once in my life, I was *glad* he had said I was too young to do something.

I could feel Bryce glaring at me. I tried to stop a

smug smile from spreading across my face, but I couldn't.

There was only a fleeting moment of satisfaction, however. Then my anxiety returned. That night was so important. I hated to admit it, but I was scared.

I thought Bryce would never leave the house. I knew he was eager to get to the Snoring, but he was hanging around to see what I was doing.

I stuck a copy of a book called *Onion Jam* in front of my face and sat on my bed with some pillows propped up behind me. Bryce kept passing my room and glancing inside.

After what seemed like forever, he went downstairs. I heard his car start and the squeal of tires as he peeled out of the driveway.

I went to the window and watched him turn right at the end of the road. It was the way to Farmer Withers's field. Then I swung into action.

The plan was for all of us to meet Prince Brassica in front of Veggie Village, which was closed. Somehow he'd have a car, and he'd drive us out to Dozer's Pharmaceutical Supply House.

Because of all the skin disorders in town, employees were loading trucks with antifungal cream around the clock. When we got to Dozer's, we would all morph into vegetables and get as big as we could. We were hoping the sight of us would terrify the employees, and we'd be able to make them drive trucks of antifungal cream out to Farmer Withers's place.

After that, we'd scare the drivers into parking the trucks and running away. Then we'd shrink down to regular vegetable size and lay low until it was time to proceed with the attack.

My heart thumped in my chest as I put my sneakers on. If we didn't stop the Jerkks here, they would just keep spreading. The fate of the earth was in our hands tonight . . . not to mention my very own life.

As I smeared myself with antifungal cream, I stared at my reflection in the mirror and tried to look like the steely heroes in action movies. But my mouth felt dry. I kept asking myself the same question over and over again. Would I save the world tonight . . . or would I just end up a Jerkk?

Chapter Nineteen

It was about eleven o'clock that night when we all met up in front of Veggie Village. I'd climbed out of my window, down the tree in the backyard, and then over the fence to get out of the house. If my parents ever knew I was out this late, they'd freak.

The rest of the group was already standing on the sidewalk in front of the darkened restaurant when I arrived.

"We were beginning to think you weren't coming," said Olivia.

"My brother kept hanging around," I told her. "He knows something's up, I can tell. He kept passing by my room and looking in like he was spying on me."

Olivia stuck her hands in the pockets of her jeans and rocked back and forth. "It really doesn't matter if your brother suspects something after tonight," she said.

Silence fell over the group. We knew she was right.

Tommy looked at his watch. "So where's Prince Brassica, anyway? He said he'd be here at ten-forty-five."

"Don't worry," Olivia told him. "I said he could use the truck from my mom and dad's greenhouse if he couldn't find anything else. We had a last-minute emergency delivery of flowers to a reception hall for a wedding tomorrow. Prince Brassica will be here."

I started babbling just to keep from jumping out of my skin. "You know what I was thinking when I sneaked out of the house tonight? That my mom and dad would go bananas if they knew I was out so late." I let out a laugh. "Can you imagine what they'd do if they knew *why* I was out so late? You'd have to peel them off the ceiling." I laughed again. This time, I just couldn't stop.

I laughed until my sides hurt. I doubled over with laughter until I thought my head would explode.

I don't think I was laughing because something was funny. I wondered if I was losing my mind.

Then I heard a horn honk. I straightened up and saw the rickety green truck that belonged to Olivia's parents. Prince Brassica was in the driver's seat.

I'm looking at a beat-up old green truck being driven by a giant stalk of broccoli, I said to myself as I sucked in a couple of deep breaths. Then I helplessly started laughing again. I could feel myself going over the edge. *La-la land, here I come*, I thought.

The door of the truck opened and slammed shut again. Prince Brassica stalked toward me. He grabbed my shoulders with his tentacles. "Get hold of yourself!" he ordered.

Tears were streaming down my cheeks. "But why? You've got hold of me!" I burbled out between guffaws.

Prince Brassica bent down and stared into my eyes. "I order you to cease laughing right now! Or I'll turn you into a Caesar salad forever."

Should I cease or Caesar? I asked myself. Now *that* struck me as funny. But for some reason, I stopped laughing. I think it was because of the powerful, hypnotic effect Prince Brassica had on me.

"Breathe deeply and think about vegetables," he said. "I want you to picture them in your mind as I say them." He began talking in a slow, steady rhythm like the tick-tock of a clock.

"Artichokes."

Tick-tock.

"Asparagus."

Tick-tock.

"Beets."

Tick-tock.

"Broccoli."

Tick-tock.

"Brussels sprouts."

Tick-tock.

"Cabbages."

Tick-tock.

"Carrots."

Tick-tock.

"Celery."

Tick-tock.

"Corn."

Tick-tock.

"Eggplants."

Tick-tock.

"Leeks."

Tick-tock.

I straightened up and took a deep breath. "I'm okay now. I thought I was losing my mind for a minute."

Prince Brassica looked me in the eye and said solemnly, "You *were* losing your mind. I was worried there for a while. I knew if I had to go all the way to *zucchini*, it was too late. Now, let's get on with the plan."

Chapter Twenty

When we got to Dozer's Pharmaceutical Supply House, the area around the loading dock was buzzing with activity. Guys in white coats and caps with DOZER embroidered on the front were loading case after case stamped with the words ANTIFUNGAL AGENT in red.

My palms were sweaty, but I wasn't losing my grip. I was all vegetable-juiced up and ready to go. When I morphed this time, I needed to be a big, tough vegetable. *Why not a rutabaga?* I decided.

"Ready to rumba?" asked Prince Brassica.

"The expression is *Ready to rumble*," said Tommy.

Prince Brassica scowled. "Don't split peas," he said. "Let's go to work!"

The royal broccoli parked the truck by the side of the building, where it was dark. We all got out quietly and, standing side by side, started to morph.

Of course, Prince Brassica remained a big broccoli. I

became a rutabaga as I had planned. The rest of the group chose to morph into their favorite vegetables. Tommy became a tomato, Randi was a radish, and Olivia was an olive. Cary, of course, was a carrot. I think he had hardly ever morphed into anything else.

I concentrated on becoming as gigantic a rutabaga as possible. My own height is five feet, five inches, which I think is okay for my age of thirteen. Besides, I've been growing like a weed.

When I opened my eyes, I was a giant purple-and-white turniplike vegetable. I had skinny, tentacle-like arms with long skinny fingers and stalklike legs with long narrow feet. I almost scared myself. I figured I would easily terrorize a poor Dozer loader.

"Wow!" Olivia said to me. "I bet you're practically seven feet tall!"

She had turned into an absolutely awesome olive. I blushed. "Thanks," I said. "I really tried to get scary."

"I think you did a great job," she replied.

"Let's not stand around making small talk that doesn't amount to a hill of beans," snapped Prince Brassica. "Let's get out there and scare 'em to death. Just make sure they get you to Withers's place before they die of fright."

We all swung into action. I waddled around the side of the building right behind Prince Brassica. I watched him go up to a guy holding a big box and just stand there.

The man let out a tomato-juice-curdling scream and threw the box into the air. Prince Brassica reached out a

99

long tentacle and grabbed him. Then he pulled him into a truck.

The prince sure didn't waste any time. *Way to go,* I thought with admiration.

I waddled over to a young, chubby-cheeked fellow with a puzzled expression on his face. He was looking around to see who had screamed, wondering what had happened.

I seized the guy from behind and threw him into the driver's seat of a truck before he knew what had hit him. His eyes grew wide and his face got as red as Tommy Tomato when he looked at me. He opened and shut his mouth several times, but he didn't make a sound. He just couldn't.

I felt sorry for the guy. I had thought I would enjoy scaring somebody, but now that I saw how terrified he was, I felt bad. But it couldn't be helped. I had to do what I had to do.

Since I didn't want to get tired out from communicating with a never-morphed human, I had written my instructions in a note.

Cooperate and you won't get squashed. Drive to Farmer Withers's field. Go left at the gate, then make a right and keep on going.

The guy's hands shook so hard when he put the key in the ignition that his bones almost rattled. But he did as he was told.

He put the pedal to the metal and practically flew down the road. The wind rushed over me through the open window. Trees, fences, and houses blurred.

We were at Farmer Withers's place in an hour, but I knew that was in vegetable time. It had been only a few minutes in human time.

When we got close to the field, I pulled out my second page of instructions:

Park in the woods at the edge of the field. Then you're free to go. Just keep quiet.

The poor guy was covered with sweat. He nodded silently and did as he was instructed.

The second we pulled to a stop, he shot out the door. I watched him running away through the woods. He was breathing so hard that I could hear him huffing and puffing.

Mine was the first truck to arrive. Off in the distance, I could see that the Snoring was in full swing.

Farmer Withers had strung little mushroomlike lights all around. Some bad seventies disco music was playing on an old, scratchy record player.

It was easy to tell that most of the members of the crowd were already Jerkks. Of course, only the rash would tell me for sure, and I couldn't see that. But I figured they were Jerkks by the way they were dressed and the way they were acting.

The field was like a big bargain-basement warehouse or a cheap clothing store. I could see just about every dopey piece of clothing ever made: Clip-on bow ties. Polyester leisure suits. High-water pants that showed skinny ankles. Vinyl shoes. Plaid golf caps with pom-poms. Some girls had butterfly clips in their hair and impossibly long, bright red nails. Some guys were in shorts with white socks pulled up to their knees.

It's almost enough to make me want to run for the nearest mail-order catalog, I thought. I scanned the crowd for my brother but didn't see him.

The wind blew, and I caught the scent of a mixture of awful fungal stench and cheap cologne. Luckily, rutabagas don't have a heightened sense of smell.

I remembered how sick I had been the first night I had smelled the fungus on this field. Now it was probably ten times worse. Combined with the cologne, I figured that if I were a human, I'd probably keel over.

Another truck pulled up beside the one my driver had just vacated. Cary got out. I motioned him over.

"Hey, Cary, I need you to use your eyes for me. I'm trying to spot my brother in the crowd. Do you see him?"

Cary began scanning the group at the Snoring. Meanwhile, his driver was running away through the woods just as mine had.

"There he is," Cary said. He gestured with a tentacle toward the far corner of the field. I could see someone there, but I never would have figured out who it was.

"Bryce is wearing a blue, short-sleeved shirt with cuffs. He has on white socks pulled up to his knees. And—I hate to tell you this, Kyle—he's wearing a clip-on bow tie, too."

"Oh, no. He really has become a Jerkk," I said sadly.

I didn't have time to dwell on thoughts of my brother. Just then two other trucks pulled up. Prince Brassica got out of one. Randi got out of the other.

The driver of Prince Brassica's truck raced off into the woods just as the other two had done. But when the driver of Randi's truck got out, he just stood there for a moment and grinned.

"Glad I could drop you off," he said to Randi. He was tall, thin, and probably not much older than twenty-one.

I started feeling uneasy. *This guy should be scared*, I thought. *Why isn't he?*

The driver took off his white coat slowly and revealed the ridiculous outfit he had on underneath: a short-sleeved, pinstriped shirt with a pocket protector full of pens. The blue stripes clashed with his bright green bow tie. I could see an awful, scaly red rash on his arms.

We were all too shocked to move as he said in a slow, threatening voice, "You see, I was planning on coming this way. I'm sure the other Jerkks will be happy to know you're here."

As we all stared in a*maize*ment, the guy pulled a sleeping bag from the back of the truck. Then he ran off *toward* the Snoring.

Chapter Twenty-One

The guy who had driven Randi's truck charged toward the crowd at the Snoring. He was pointing and shouting. The Jerkks began turning in our direction.

That's when things really started to rock and roll. The crowd charged us, throwing rocks and the rolls they had been dunking in their mushroom soup—an angry hoard wearing mismatched outfits.

The trucks driving Tommy and Olivia pulled up as the rest of us were ripping open cases of antifungal cream. Thankfully, these drivers clearly weren't Jerkks. One ran off into the woods. The other one fainted.

In seconds, the fungus-infested Jerkks had reached us. By then we had armed ourselves with tubes of antifungal cream. Each of us stood by open boxes that contained many more. As the Jerkks got close, we aimed our tubes and squeezed hard.

Splat!

Splat!
Splatsplatsplatsplatsplat!

Globs and blobs of antifungal cream went flying through the air in all directions. Even in the midst of my frenzy and fear, it reminded me of one of those food fights you see in the movies.

I squirted and zapped, squirted and zapped, squirted and zapped. I think the zapping was what kept me from falling down from exhaustion. It came naturally to me, just as Prince Brassica had said it would. And it was energizing. The more I zapped, the more I glowed with vitamins and minerals.

As the antifungal cream hit the human Jerkks, they howled with anger. As they were zapped, they cried out in pain.

Then an incredible thing happened. The people began to snap out of their trances as if waking from dreams. They began to rub the antifungal cream on their rashes. They kicked off their shoes wildly and smeared it all over their infected feet.

Some of them screamed again, this time in horror, when they saw what they were wearing. Especially the girls.

"How totally embarrassing!" shrieked one of them named Emily, who had been in my biology class the year before. She was dressed in a beige pleated skirt with an elasticized waistband. On her baggy blouse was a smiley-face pin. Tears began streaming down her cheeks, and she practically tore out clumps of long blonde hair.

Other more serious types began shouting their thanks to us. "I didn't even know who I was," said a man I recognized from the library. "It was like I was trapped in a bad movie, and I was the star!" He and many others grabbed tubes of antifungal cream and began trying to help us in our fight.

It was a good thing, too, because then the real villains came at us. The Streptococci, the Trichophyton, and the worst Jerkks of all—the dreaded Rubrum fungi.

My heart nearly stopped beating. Imagine an army of science fiction monsters more than ten feet tall coming after little ol' *you*. They were frightening to look at and awful to smell.

The Streptococci staggered along. They were almost like lacy party doilies, except for their three gigantic, furious eyes, each reaching out on the end of a claw. They looked pretty scary, but my friends and I *wokked* them right and left. I gave two of them a few good swift kicks. We got the Strep soldiers out of the way pretty fast, but they were nothing compared with the Trichophyton fungus. The Trichophyton were an angry red color and full of oozing pus.

The Rubrum came at us last. They were the biggest and the most horrifying. Basically they were huge masses of ugly, smelly tentacles.

The fungi began attacking and phagocytosing their victims. Remember what I said that word meant? *Engulfing* them. Smothering them. Consuming them.

I wanted to turn and run, but then I heard the screams of pain from the people who had already been infected by the Rubrum. They were still on Farmer Withers's field. They groaned and scratched and begged for help.

"This itching is driving me insane! Help! Help!" screamed one of them. I recognized his voice. It was my brother. In spite of my terror, I kept on squirting and zapping.

When the antifungal cream hit the fungi, I couldn't believe what happened. I could actually see the antifungal agents attacking. They sprang out of the cream and quickly multiplied.

They were orange creatures. Many of them were as big as the Rubrum, and they had as many tentacles.

All over the field, antifungal agents and Rubrum wrestled. They roared at each other in fury.

For a single, wonderful moment I thought we were actually winning. Then I saw the most awful thing I've ever seen in my life.

A gigantic Rubrum fungus smothered Cary. In an instant, the mass of tentacles covered him. He never had a chance.

I tried to run to help him, but it was already too late. And that's when the rainstorm started.

Chapter Twenty-Two

It was morning. Somehow I was in my bedroom, and I had woken up with a headache. Actually, I found out later that it wasn't the *next* morning at all, but the one after that. I had slept for more than twenty-four hours.

The sun was streaming through my window. I could hear birds singing. The horror of what had happened seemed impossible. But I knew *it had happened.*

The rainstorm was the worst that had ever hit our town. Water poured from the sky. Wind lashed the trees and blew sheets of rain so dense that they actually hurt. The sky turned so dark that I couldn't see my hand in front of me.

I slowly began to recall Prince Brassica gathering me, Randi, Olivia, and Tommy into one of the trucks and driving. But I don't remember how I actually made it home and wound up in my own bed.

Then it hit me. Cary was gone—forever. I wasn't sure what else had actually happened, but I was about to find out. I heard a knock at the door.

"Come in," I called.

The door opened, and Bryce came into the room. "Hi, dork," he said. Then he smiled.

I scrunched back against the headboard. Bryce the Jerkk was still here!

Or was he? Bryce was shaking his head. "Look, I know what you're thinking, but I'm not a Jerkk. It's really me. I'm okay, except for this. . . ." He held out his hands. My mouth dropped open. His nails—they were yellowish and greenish.

The Rubrum got him, I thought.

"It's okay, really. Dad's treating this with antifungal cream. And there are some new pills. So the fungus won't control me. I'll be me, not a Jerkk."

Then Bryce smiled again. "I always was a bit of a *jerk* before, though. I was a lousy brother. Things will be different now, I promise. I know what you did for me, and for everyone, including the vegetables. You're a hero."

My eyes widened. I didn't know what to believe.

Bryce raked his hands through his hair and sat down on the edge of my bed. "Do you want to know what happened after you left?"

I nodded.

"Everything." Bryce said. "It rained so hard that the bacteria and the fungus that were left were destroyed. Farmer Withers's field is destroyed, too." Bryce twisted his mouth into an expression of disgust. "It's gross," he said. "It's a mess of mud and antifungal cream. Nothing will ever grow there again. But at least that's better than what was growing there for a little while. Anyway, I don't work there anymore. Farmer Withers left town."

The two of us sat there briefly in silence. "I'd like to be alone for a while, please," I said. I was glad that the fungus hadn't taken over, but it didn't mean I was *happy*.

"Okay," Bryce said. "I guess you've got a lot to think about." He left the room and closed the door behind him.

I put my head in my hands. All I could think about was Cary—what a wonderful, unusual, brilliant person he had been.

Then I heard a voice. "Pssst! Open the window!"

I turned in the direction of the voice. At first I didn't see anything, but when I did, my heart leaped with joy. There was a *carrot* sitting on my windowsill!

The carrot spoke again. "Come on, don't just sit there. Open up. It's me. Cary!"

I nearly flew out of bed and pushed open the window. "I can't believe you're alive!" I said. "I was sure that—"

"I know," said Cary as his orange body hopped into the room. "You thought I was a goner. So did I, until Prince Brassica saved me. I never saw a zap like the one he gave that Rubrum. It was like a lightning bolt. The thing was toast."

I could hardly keep from jumping up and down, I

was so happy. Now Cary, Tommy, Randi, Olivia, and I could be friends together, just as before. But something puzzled me.

"Cary . . . why don't you morph back?"

The carrot was silent for a moment. Then Cary looked at me with an expression I'd never seen on a carrot before. "I can't," he said. "It's too complicated to explain, but the only way I can stay alive now is in the body you see here."

I was stunned and felt like I was going to faint.

Cary hopped over to me. "It's really okay, Kale. I mean *Kyle*." Cary smiled. "I *like* being a carrot. You know, I never was very happy at home. Mom was always out shopping, and all Dad ever did was read weight-lifting magazines. I'm better off where I am. I live with Prince Brassica and his family under Withers's field now."

Cary turned a darker shade of orange. "The whole place is a mess. Between the antifungal cream and the mud—well, we're going to be working around the clock to clean things up."

"I guess that means I won't see you much," I said sadly.

"Well . . . not as much as before. I've got a different life now. Listen, I've got to go, but I'll stop by sooner than you think. I'll see Randi, Tommy, and Olivia, too. And I'll always be thinking of you." Cary hopped back up on the windowsill.

"It's *so long* for now," he said. "But not *good-bye*. Look at your answering machine."

I turned and saw that the message light was flashing. When I looked back at the window, Cary was gone.

I let out a long sigh and pressed the button on the answering machine. I heard Prince Brassica's deep green voice.

"You fought well. But no matter what you hear, don't believe anyone who says the fight is over. We hurt the Jerkks badly, but we didn't stamp out athlete's foot and other rashes completely."

The hair on my head stood up. My hands gripped the answering machine.

"Fun Gus and some other fungi and bacteria are around. They're just dormant. That means they're hibernating—recovering, waiting to strike. It might not be soon, but strike again they will."

I gritted my teeth. My friends and I would keep fighting them until we won.

"I've got to remain underground for a while now," I heard Prince Brassica say. "My family and I are well, though. I'll take care of Cary. And someday I'll be in touch."

There was a pause and then I heard, "This tape will self-destruct in five seconds."

I let go of the answering machine as if it were a hot potato. A thin wisp of smoke drifted up from it.

I blinked and shook my head. Everything that had happened had me all shaken up. But one thing was certain: If the fungi and bacteria ever returned, the Vegemorphs would be ready!